Dear Reader,

Home, family, community and love. These are the values we cherish most in our lives—the ideals that ground us, comfort us, move us. They certainly provide the perfect inspiration around which to build a romance collection that will touch the heart.

And so we are thrilled to offer you the Harlequin Heartwarming series. Each of these special stories is a wholesome, heartfelt romance imbued with the traditional values so important to you. They are books you can share proudly with friends and family. And the authors featured in this collection are some of the most talented storytellers writing today, including favorites such as Tara Taylor Quinn, Janice Kay Johnson, Jillian Hart and Shelley Galloway. We've selected these stories especially for you based on their overriding qualities of emotion and tenderness, and they center around your favorite themes—children, weddings, second chances, the reunion of families, the quest to find a true home and, of course, sweet romance.

So curl up in your favorite chair, relax and prepare for a heartwarming reading experience!

Sincerely,

The Editors

LORI HANDELAND

is a *New York Times, USA TODAY,* Waldenbooks and BookScan bestselling author and the recipient of many industry awards, including two RITA® Awards from Romance Writers of America for Best Paranormal (*Blue Moon*) and Best Long Contemporary Romance (*The Mommy Quest*), an *RT Book Reviews* Award for Best Harlequin Superromance (*A Soldier's Quest*), a Colorado Romance Writers Award of Excellence, a Write Touch Readers Award, a National Readers Choice Award and a Prism Award.

Lori is published worldwide in several genres—historical, contemporary, series and paranormal romance, as well as urban fantasy and historical fantasy. She lives in Wisconsin with her husband, enjoying occasional visits from her grown sons. She loves to hear from readers and can be reached at LHANDEL120@aol.com.

New York Times Bestselling Author

Lori Handeland

A Mom for Tim

⊕ HARLEQUIN®
entertain, enrich, inspire™

Recycling programs
for this product may
not exist in your area.

ISBN-13: 978-0-373-36571-5

A MOM FOR TIM

Copyright © 2012 by Lori Handeland

Originally published as THE MOMMY QUEST
Copyright © 2006 by Lori Handeland

A Mom for Tim

For my mommy—Beverley Jo Miller.
I couldn't have found a better one if
I'd gone on a quest of my own.
Love you!

CHAPTER ONE

"HEY, LUCHETTI! IF THAT'S really your name."

Laughter broke out on the playground. Tim glanced up from his own private game of football. In his world he was Aaron Rodgers throwing a touchdown pass to win the Super Bowl.

Of course, he never told anyone how much he loved Aaron. He lived in Illinois, land of Lincoln and the Chicago Bears. If he said Rodgers was the greatest quarterback of all time, he just might get a bloody nose.

Tim eyed the circle of boys who'd suddenly decided to pay attention to him, but not in a nice way, and thought he might end up with a bloody nose, anyway. Even though they were laughing, they looked big and mean and ready to stop laughing real soon.

Tim had been in this situation before. When bullies came it was best to hide and get small. Except he was gettin' really tired of hiding. Besides, his father had told him he never had to worry about people hurting him again. Not in Gainsville. Not while Dean Luchetti was around.

Too bad he wasn't around right now.

"My name's Luchetti," Tim insisted. "Just like my dad's."

The leader, Jeremy Janquist, a kid so big everyone secretly figured he'd been held back, stepped away from his buddies with a sneer. "He isn't really your dad. He just took you in when you showed up in the yard."

That was kind of true. Except Dean was adopting him, and then they'd be a family forevermore.

"My name's Luchetti," Tim repeated.

"Say that on your birth certificate, dim bulb?"

Tim winced, then wished he hadn't when Jeremy grinned. He had problems in school, not because he was dim, but because he had a tough time payin' attention. Even if there weren't so many fun things to see and do in any given day, sittin' still was hard!

Tim tried to walk away as his new gramma had told him to do when kids teased, but Jeremy wasn't the kind of guy you turned your back on.

"Moron." Jeremy grabbed Tim's arm and spun him around. His fingers seemed to crunch against Tim's bones.

Tim's hands automatically curled into fists. He'd lived on the streets before he came to Illinois; he'd faced bigger, meaner kids than Jeremy. If he had to, he could fight. But he sure hoped he wouldn't have to.

"Do you even have a birth certificate? I hear you ate garbage. That your mom hated you so much she dumped you in an alley and took off. You made up your first name, stole your last one, and you don't even know when your birthday is."

Jeremy had heard right, but Tim wasn't going to tell him so. Tim wasn't going to tell him anything. He tightened his lips along with his fists and counted to ten.

Sadly his silence only seemed to make Jeremy's friends brave. They inched closer and started to shout.

"Loser."

"No name."

"Stupid."

"Hyper."

"Dumpster baby."

Tim's eyes stung with the effort of holding back the rage and the tears. Every single one of those names was true.

Still, he yelled, "Am not!"

Someone shoved Tim from behind. He stumbled into a boy directly in front of him who shoved right back. Tim fell, landing on his knees. He scrambled to his feet, knowing if he was down they might kick, or worse, but as Tim got up someone's shoulder met his face. The bloody nose he'd expected began.

Tim glanced around to see if the blood would scare them, or only make them madder. Every single boy was bigger than Tim, who wasn't very big at all.

His dad said he'd catch up to all the other kids, just look at his feet. Tim's feet were huge, which was why he tripped a lot.

"You don't even have a mom," Jeremy sneered.

"Do, too."

She was just…gone. Tim didn't remember a thing about the woman who had left him somewhere, then never come back.

"Only losers don't have moms."

Tim had Dean—the daddy he'd found when he'd gone on his daddy quest. He had aunts, uncles, cousins and the best gramma and grampa in the world, who lived right across the cornfield. Everyone loved him. On the farm, Tim wasn't an orphan, he was a Luchetti.

But most kids had moms, even if she didn't live with them. They knew their mom's name, where she was, why she'd left.

Most kids, but not Tim.

"I don't need a mom," Tim muttered.

"That's good, because you ain't gonna get one. Loser."

Jeremy headed for the open area behind

the school, where the other boys were playing real football. Tim breathed a sigh of relief that he'd avoided getting punched or landing in trouble. Then Jeremy tossed one final taunt over his shoulder.

"I hear your dad is as big of a dimwit as you are. No one'll marry him."

"What did you say?"

The playground went silent. Was every kid staring at them?

Jeremy came back, towering over Tim, wearing a nasty grin that said he'd been waiting for this. "I *said* your dad is an idiot. The only job he could get is bein' a farmer, and that's because his dad gave him the farm. He's never been married, 'cause he can't get a girl, and he had to adopt a kid that was as dumb as an old cow, just like him."

Tim stopped listenin' to Gramma Ellie's advice and moved on to his dad's. *When all else fails...*

Tim socked Jeremy as hard as he could in his big, soft belly. While Jeremy writhed on the ground, Tim said quietly, "Don't ever talk about my dad again."

He lifted his gaze and the others shrank back. Tim might be little, but he'd lived in a place where meaner kids than this had tried to do a lot worse. And no one, *no one,* talked about his dad like that.

Tim left Jeremy on the pavement with his friends gathered around. He ignored the other children and headed toward the school, where he took a seat against the building and dabbed at his nose with his shirt.

Someone would come and take him to the principal's office. They always did.

Until he'd met Dean Luchetti, Tim had never known love or home or family. He'd do anything for Dean.

Tim sat up straight, focusing on his idea. Why hadn't he thought of this before? He'd prove everyone wrong. He'd find Dean a wife and himself a mother.

The time had come for the mommy quest.

"STELLA? I MEAN, Ms. O'Connell?"

Stella lifted her head and waited for Laura Benedict, her administrative assistant, to get on with it. Instead, the woman just stared at her.

"Yes?" Stella tried to keep the impatience out of her voice and failed.

She had to remember that she was new here. Well, not new, exactly. She'd attended this school. But she was the new *principal* of Gainsville Elementary.

She just needed time to get used to how things were done in Illinois, which was different than they'd been done in Los Angeles. Some of those changes were the result of working in an elementary school in the Midwest, rather than a high school in the center of one of the largest cities in the country, and then again some weren't.

"I'm sorry," Laura said. "I keep forgetting and calling you Stella. It's just, I remember you that way."

Laura had been a year behind Stella at Gainsville High. Now she was the mother of four preteen boys, the wife of a farmer and the admin assistant at the grade school.

Laura had been one of the popular girls. Once slim and lovely, she was now round and cute. She was also happy. Or at least

Stella thought she was. She'd seen so few happy people over the past several years.

"Stella?" Laura made an annoyed sound deep in her throat. "I mean, Ms. O'Connell."

"Never mind, Laura. Just tell me what you want."

Her admin blinked at Stella's tone. She'd been too abrupt again. Would she ever be able to fit into the slower, kinder, gentler world of Gainsville Elementary? Stella was having her doubts.

"There's been a fight on the playground."

Stella came to her feet. "Is an ambulance on the way? Were shots fired?"

Laura's eyes widened, and she stared at Stella with both confusion and horror.

"Sorry," Stella muttered. "Wrong time zone. What happened?"

"You get to find out."

"I do?"

In L.A. she'd had assistants for that. By the time the students reached her office, they'd not only been interviewed, they'd usually been booked.

"We've got one in the nurse's office with

a bellyache the size of the Willis Tower. The other's cooling his heels at my desk waiting to talk to you."

"Swell."

"Just ask him what happened," Laura said. "Being sent to the principal's office is enough to get most kids to spill their guts."

"Okay." Stella sat down.

"Oh." Laura stopped half in and half out of the door, eyeing Stella's favorite suit, a light shade that brought out the auburn highlights in her short, dark hair and the green in her hazel eyes. "Don't hug him— he's kind of bloody."

Hug him?

Stella was still pondering those words when the child walked into her office. He didn't look scared; he looked like a refugee from her world.

Short, skinny, with huge feet and knobby, scraped knees, there was something in those blue eyes she recognized. This child had been beat on before.

Stella frowned. "Have a seat."

Someone, probably Laura, had tried to wipe the blood off his face. But noses bled pretty badly, and his white T-shirt was now garbage. She'd have to ask Laura to get him a new one from the donation box. Parents tended to freak out when they saw their children covered in blood.

"What's your name?"

"Rat."

"What?" The word erupted from Stella's mouth—too loud and too sharp for little kids. But this one didn't even flinch. He'd no doubt heard worse.

"Rug Rat, really." He shrugged his bony shoulders, and his hair, which reached past his eyes, slid over the freckles dotting his bloody nose. "But they called me Rat."

"Who are they?"

"Don't remember."

If he was hosing her, he was good. Still, she couldn't fathom anyone in Gainsville being able to call a kid Rat and get away with it.

"Laura?" Stella's assistant stuck her head in the door. "He says his name is Rat."

Laura made an exasperated sound. "Tim, do you want to be in more trouble than you are?"

"No, ma'am," he answered, but he kept his gaze fixed on Stella's.

"Call his parents," Stella murmured.

"Already done."

If she hadn't been locking eyes with Tim, she wouldn't have caught the slight wince.

"Wanna tell me what happened out there?" Stella asked.

"Nope."

"Who punched you in the nose?"

"I fell."

"Funny, I hear that a lot."

"I fall a lot."

"There's a kid in the nurse's office with stomach issues. Know anything about that?"

"He fell, too."

Stella lifted an eyebrow. "Someone's going to tattle. They won't be able to help themselves. Then I'll know everything. You could save us both time."

"Someone can tattle, but it ain't gonna be me."

Tim folded his arms over his chest, revealing livid, finger-shaped bruises on his left forearm.

Her eyes narrowed and her temper flared. There was one thing that never changed no matter the time zone.

Some parents liked to hurt their kids.

DEAN LUCHETTI TOSSED a hay bale onto the wagon and caught sight of his mother waving from the end of the field. His dad saw her, too, and shut off the tractor. Together they removed their seed caps and wiped their foreheads.

September and the thermometer read eighty degrees. In Illinois, the weather changed as often as the direction of the wind. One of the many things Dean loved about it.

"What's the matter, Ellie?" John asked.

Dean started in her direction. She wouldn't come out here unless it was important.

"School called."

Dean's breath caught in his throat as his heart took a leap upward.

"He's fine," she said hurriedly, and Dean relaxed a bit. With Tim *fine* was usually the best he could hope for.

Dean had fallen in love with the little boy almost from the instant they'd met. His mom said they went together like peas and carrots—different, yet somehow they fit.

Tim had no one; Dean needed someone. When they'd both been diagnosed with ADHD some of Dean's troubles had been explained, and Tim had found a father who could understand him better than anyone else.

"What is it this time?" Dean asked.

"Fight."

"Someone hit him?" Dean's voice was so loud he startled a few birds from the nearby trees.

"I don't know who hit who first," his mom said. "But according to Laura, you should see the other guy."

Dean stopped. "Really?"

"Don't sound so proud. You need to get to school. He's suspended."

"Shh—ucky darns."

Dean had been trying to quit swearing, since Tim repeated everything he said. Giving up smoking had gone a whole lot better.

"I'll finish here."

Dean glanced at his mom. "Leave it. You can't lift those bales."

Her answer was a snort. "Right. I was lifting hay bales when you were still a gleam in your daddy's eye."

Dean glanced at his father, who was sitting on the tractor staring at the sky, and if Dean knew him at all, wishing for the days when he would have had a lit cigarette in his hand. A heart attack several years back had ended not only his love affair with nicotine, but also with alcohol, red meat and the daily workings of his farm.

Dean's mother came from sturdy stock. Eleanor Luchetti had birthed six children in seven years, raising them all with one iron hand while she helped his father with the other. But they were semiretired now, and she had no business out in the heat doing Dean's job.

"Leave it," he repeated. "Tim can help me since he'll be free this afternoon."

"Tim's in second grade and weighs sixty pounds soaking wet."

"But he works like a dog."

"He does." Eleanor smiled. She was almost as crazy about Tim as Dean was.

Dean strode toward the thresher's cottage on the far side of a cornfield that separated the house where he now lived from the house where he'd grown up. As soon as he entered the yard, a herd of dogs surrounded him.

His mother was right; having five dogs was pushing it. Of course, they used to have eight.

"Move your kids," Dean muttered.

Bear, one of an original pair of dalmatians named for the Luchettis' favorite sports teams, knew that tone. A herder at heart, he ushered his four remaining offspring toward the backfield.

Bear's love affair with a French poodle had resulted in six fluffy, spotted puppies, known as doodles. Dean had managed to foist two of them off on his brothers. He hadn't had a speck of luck with the rest.

The second dalmatian, Bull, had recently completed an affair of his own with a Mexican mutt by the name of Lucky. Bull had chosen to move to Quintana Roo with the love of his life and their flock of puppies, dubbed mutations since they were so ugly they were cute.

With the dancing, prancing dogs out of the way, Dean was able to make it into his house. He considered taking a shower, but opted for a quick wash in the sink and a change of his T-shirt instead.

A veteran principal's-office sitter himself, Dean didn't want Tim incarcerated there any longer than necessary, so he snatched the keys to his red pickup from the nail on the wall and headed for town.

School had been hard on Dean. He'd never been able to sit still, hadn't cared about reading or math; he'd only been interested in the land and the animals.

Twenty-seven years ago there'd been no testing, no special classes, no mainstreaming. You either made it through school or you didn't. Dean had made it, but just barely.

These days kids had the benefits of special education, extra funding, medication—things Dean had once considered a bunch of namby-pamby nonsense—until Tim came along.

He wheeled into the parking lot of Gainsville Elementary and hopped out of the cab. The place hadn't changed much since he'd attended classes here, which meant it had a lot in common with the rest of the town.

Not that Gainsville hadn't changed—there was a brand-new hospital and quite a few new businesses—but in truth, the same people ran the place that always had. And if not them, then their kids. Just look at him.

Dean strode into the building and headed for the office, nodding to the volunteer parent aide seated just inside the door.

Times *had* changed since he'd last been here—not a big surprise. Gone were the days when you could just walk off the street and into a classroom to talk to your child. Even in Nowhere, Illinois, they'd had to institute school security.

Although he doubted Chloe Wrycroft, five foot two and eyes of blue, would be able to stop anyone from going anywhere that they wanted to if they wanted to badly enough. Still, she had a high-pitched shrieky voice that had already deafened her husband and would no doubt arouse the entire school if she chose to use it. At least no one would be surprised by an attack.

The thought was so disturbing Dean shoved it from his mind as he pushed through the door into the main office. Laura Benedict lifted her gaze from the computer with a tense smile.

Dean frowned. Laura was usually so cheery.

"What happened?" he demanded.

She glanced at the closed door that read Principal. Then inched to the counter and lowered her voice. "Near as I can piece together, some boys were teasing Tim."

"About what?" Dean asked, but he already knew.

"Being dumb, being an orphan—"

Dean rolled his eyes.

Laura flashed him a glare. They'd known each other since they were younger than Tim, and she always spoke to him as if she were his sister. Then again, she spoke to everyone that way. "Dean…"

"Where is he?"

"With her."

"You left him alone with Mrs. Little?"

The principal of Gainsville Elementary resembled Mary Poppins, until she opened her mouth. Then she was more like the Attila the Hun. Mrs. Little had frightened generations of boys and girls. He didn't plan to let her continue with his son.

But Laura was staring at him as if he'd lost his marbles. "Don't you remember?"

"Remember what?"

"Mrs. Little fell off her high heels and ripped her Achilles tendon."

"So she's meaner than usual?"

"She's retired."

Dean blinked. Now that Laura mentioned it, he did recall seeing something about that in the *Gainsville Gazette.*

"So who's in there?"

As if his question had summoned the occupant, the door began to open.

"Dean, I thought you knew," Laura whispered.

He glanced at her. "Knew what?"

Laura's gaze shifted and his followed.

Dean froze at the sight of the woman in the doorway.

"Stella," he said. "What are you doing here?"

CHAPTER TWO

"ME?" STELLA SNAPPED. "What about you?"

She glanced at Laura, who frowned and said, "I thought you knew."

"Knew what?"

"Dad?" Tim said from the doorway.

Ah, Stella thought. *That.*

She'd understood she would see Dean eventually; she just hadn't figured on seeing him so soon, or so *here.* She definitely hadn't figured on him being the father of one of her students. But she should have considered that, if he were, Dean would be the father of a difficult one.

Nature? Nurture? Either way, trouble usually showed up in the next generation.

In this case, however, Stella had the distinct feeling the incident with the other boys hadn't been all Tim's fault. Not because Tim was adorable, and Dean's, but because after six years in various school systems, she knew when something smelled fishy even without using her nose. The explanations of every child involved reeked.

She glanced at Tim, whose stained shirt, which he hadn't had time to change, made him resemble an escapee from a war zone. Even Stella, who'd already had the nurse determine the boy was fine, wanted to fetch him an ice pack and call 911.

He crossed the short distance and stood in front of Dean. "I messed up."

"What the…?" Dean's fists clenched, his mouth tightened.

Stella took two quick steps forward so she could put herself between them if she needed to. If Dean wanted to punch someone, better her than his son.

He seemed to struggle with his temper. Dean had never been big on patience. She remembered that well—along with too many other things. The taste of his kiss, the scent of his hair, the bulge of his biceps against the palms of her hands.

"Let's discuss this in my office," Stella blurted.

Dean glanced up, noticed her defensive position and cursed.

Tim held out his hand. Without missing a beat, Dean reached into the pocket of his dusty jeans and pulled out a quarter.

Noticing Stella's curious expression, Dean shrugged sheepishly. "Not supposed to swear."

The two of them stared at each other, uncertain what to say. Hadn't they said it all fourteen years ago? Or had they said anything back then besides goodbye?

"Ahem." Laura cleared her throat pointedly. "Jeremy's parents will be here soon."

"Yes. Right." Stella took a breath to calm herself, then got back to work. "Stay with Mrs. Benedict, Tim, while I talk to your father."

As she said the last word, Stella fought a wince at the thought of Dean being with another woman. Not that she hadn't dated other men, but that was beside the point.

Distracted, she stumbled over the carpet in her office.

Dean grabbed her elbow. "Watch it or you'll end up like Mrs. Little."

He released her right away to shut the door, but the slight touch, impersonal as it was, flustered her even more. Her suit coat covered her completely, yet she could still feel the heat of his skin and the scrape of his calluses. Once the door was shut, the room was too small for Stella and Dean and all of the memories.

The man was still as handsome as ever. Of the five Luchetti brothers none could be called homely, however Dean was down-right gorgeous. What a waste to keep him down on the farm.

The sun and wind had drawn lines on his face that hadn't been there in high school. His eyes were still a bright clear blue, his hair dark, his skin tanned. He was tall, lanky, with broad shoulders and rough hands. A hardworking man in a lazy man's world.

Why did she find that more attractive than a college degree and a thousand-dollar suit?

Stella escaped behind her desk. "Your wife couldn't come?"

The instant the words left her mouth, she

wanted to take them back. Even though the question was a legitimate one, she had no desire to hear about the woman who'd captured the heart she'd always coveted.

"I'm not married."

Her gaze went to his left hand, but the lack of a ring meant nothing these days. Especially to a farmer who could get such things caught in a machine and lose a finger for such sentimentality.

"Don't you have a file on Tim?" he continued. "Didn't Laura fill you in on what's been happening since you left?"

The idea that she would have been gossiping over coffee with her assistant about Dean Luchetti was as insulting as it was mortifying.

"I've got better things to worry about than what you've been doing," she muttered.

"Ditto."

"Why don't you save us a few minutes and fill me in?"

"I'm adopting Tim."

Stella frowned. "Adopting? As in, haven't adopted him yet?"

"Soon."

"Then his name's not Luchetti."

"What?" Dean shouted, and Stella flinched. "Sorry," he said more quietly.

Dean had always been loud, boisterous, full of life. That was one of the things she'd loved about him.

Stella was an only child of older parents. Her household had been so quiet. She'd sapped up the energy and the sheer noise of Dean and his huge family like a camel that had found an oasis in the middle of the Sahara.

"The kids who were teasing Tim, said his name wasn't Luchetti." Stella had gotten that much out of one of Jeremy's cohorts. "He took offense."

"Why shouldn't he?"

"He hit Jeremy Janquist so hard the boy couldn't get up under his own power."

"Really?" Dean smirked.

"It's not funny. I know you and your brothers thought fighting was entertaining—"

"What else was there to do on a rainy spring afternoon?"

Stella's eyes flicked to his, recalling all the rainy afternoons they'd shared. Her father at the bank working, her mother playing bridge. Stella had been Dean's math tutor, but he'd been the one to teach her about love.

"Fighting isn't allowed in school," she snapped.

"From the looks of my son, he wasn't the only kid throwing punches. And if I remember the Janquist boy, he's a muscle-headed beast who shouldn't be allowed out of his cage—just like his father."

"Be that as it may, they're both suspended."

"Fine by me." Dean stood.

"Before you go, we need to discuss those bruises."

Dean glanced down at his hands. "Bruises?"

"On Tim. I'm going to have to call social services."

Slowly Dean lifted his gaze to hers. "You think I hurt him?"

"Did you?"

"No." His voice was quiet, but she sensed the fury bubbling just below the surface.

Stella waited for the panic that had made her leave L.A. The fear of violence that had taken away the job she'd loved, but it didn't come.

She trusted Dean. She always had. Nevertheless, her job was to ask about the bruises.

"There are bruises on his arm," Stella said.

"Tim falls a lot, runs into things, too."

"That's what they all say."

"Maybe they all fall." Dean sighed. "Tim's accident-prone, excitable, rash—a tad hyper."

"Attention deficit hyperactivity disorder," Stella muttered.

"Give the girl a gold star."

ADHD explained a few things about Tim but not everything.

"The marks are on his forearm, and they're finger shaped."

Dean scowled. "Someone grabbed him, shook him?"

"You tell me."

"I never touched the kid, except—" He tilted his head as if listening to a voice no one else could hear. "He took a header off the barn fence. I grabbed him before he kissed mud. Left arm?"

"Yes."

"Guess it was me." Dean held out his wrists. "Take me away, Miss O'Connell. Or is it Mrs. Something Else?"

"It's Ms."

Dean snorted. "How'd you end up back in Gainsville? I thought you were going to take the world by storm."

"I did," she said shortly, and that was all she planned to say about that.

"So you're an elementary school principal?" Dean's voice was incredulous.

Her eyes narrowed. "You got a problem with that?"

"No. I mean, well…" He took a deep breath. "You're a genius, Stella. What are you doing here?"

She kept asking herself the same question.

Since childhood Stella had loved books—reading them, talking about them, touching them, owning them—so despite excelling at math and science, she'd gotten a doctorate in English. But what jobs existed around books besides publishing, where you made no money, and law, where you made no friends?

Teaching, of course.

"For the past several years," she said, "I've been the principal of a high school in L.A."

Dean made a face. "Rough."

He didn't know the half of it.

"I always figured you'd wind up a brain surgeon or maybe an astronaut."

"You never…?" Stella cut off the question before she could utter it.

Of course he'd never asked her parents where she was, or what she'd become. Her father hated Dean.

She really couldn't blame him. Coming home early one day with a splitting headache to find the town bad boy kissing your valedictorian daughter would make any man murderous.

The incident had led to the two of them sneaking around for the rest of the summer, which had only added fuel to the fire in her opinion. She'd been unable to resist the danger, the intrigue…and let's face it, the kisses. No one had ever made her feel the same since.

She'd had a fairly serious relationship in grad school—been engaged and everything. But Brad had gotten a job in Texas, and she'd had her job in L.A., and, in truth, her job had meant more to her than he did. Which didn't make the basis for a good marriage.

Stella's cheeks heated. How could she be sitting here remembering how Dean had made her feel while he was waiting for her to explain how she'd wound up as the principal of Dinky Town Elementary in Podunk, U.S.A.?

"I like helping people," she said shortly. "I'm good at it, and I'm good at running things."

"You always were," he murmured. "Student council, the yearbook, prom committee."

She'd had to organize the prom. It was the only way she'd gotten to go.

"I took a temporary job teaching high school," Stella continued. "Loved it. Kept moving up and voilà—I was a principal."

He tilted his head. "Doesn't school start in L.A. right about now, too?"

"I'm on a leave of absence. My father asked me to take Mrs. Little's place until a permanent replacement can be found."

All of that was the truth, albeit with a lot of omissions. Omissions she didn't plan on filling in.

"Don't you have to have a license or something?"

"My dad was able to get the requirement waived for the time being."

"Helps to have a dad on the school board."

"Or hurts," she muttered.

Her father was mortified she'd lowered herself to be a "nose wiper," as he referred to teachers of every level. A somewhat disturbing opinion for a school board member.

However, she'd discovered there were a lot of people who ran for the school board who were more interested in the power they could wield in the community than any good they could do.

"I'll make a note of the bruises and their origin in Tim's file," she continued.

"If you have to—"

"I do."

Dean shrugged. "When can he come back to school?"

"Day after tomorrow." Stella tilted her head. "Will he be upset?"

"He'll be thrilled. I've never understood why you people think it's a punishment to send kids home. The only ones who'd be worried about missing class are the ones who'd never get sent home in the first place."

He had a point.

"Maybe you should run for the school board," she said.

"Yeah, me and your dad would have a grand old time."

Her father *did* know how to hold a grudge. She doubted he'd ever forgive her for not becoming the first woman president of the United States.

Stella followed Dean to the door. "If you need anything—" she began.

He turned quickly, almost bumping into her. Taking a step back, she tripped over the same lump in the carpet.

This time he grabbed both of her elbows to keep her from falling. Stella caught her breath. His gaze lingered on her lips, and for a second she thought he might kiss her. For a second, she wanted him to.

He released her so suddenly, Stella had to focus on not losing her balance.

"I won't be needing anything from you, Ms. O'Connell."

She could still feel the heat of his hands, a sharp contrast to the chill in his voice. What was *he* so mad about?

Dean reached for the doorknob, and she flashed fourteen years into their past.

"You told me you never wanted to see me again," she whispered.

He hesitated, and for an instant she thought he might speak. Then he just shook his head and walked out.

The night before she'd left for college they'd met on the football field to say goodbye. Instead Stella had told Dean she'd stay in Gainsville—marry him, have his children, become a farm wife.

She remembered the hope and the love that had filled her as she'd said the words, then the mortification and the pain when he'd laughed and said she'd been a fling, nothing more. None of the pretty party girls had been willing to put up with his broody, moody disposition for long. Not when there were four other Luchetti brothers who were a lot less trouble.

But Stella had been drawn to Dean's darkness. She'd thought she could bring him into the light. Just as she'd thought she could bring so many others.

She hadn't been any more right about them than she'd been about Dean.

"COME ON, KID, YOU'RE sprung," Dean said.

Tim didn't have to be told twice. He jumped up from the chair next to Laura and danced out the door on Dean's heels.

"Am I in really bad trouble?" Tim asked once they were in the truck.

"Who started it?"

"Not me. No, sir. Uh-uh."

Tim started bouncing. Luckily the seat belt kept him from hitting the ceiling.

"Try to walk away?"

"That's when I got this."

Tim held up his right arm, where new finger-size bruises had begun to form. Dean rubbed his forehead.

"How about talking to them?"

Tim pointed to his skinned knees, then to his bloody nose.

"The guy gave you a bloody nose, then you slugged him?"

Tim squirmed, looked out the window, up at the sky, down at his shoes. "Not exactly."

"You didn't slug someone?"

"I did. But he wasn't the one who gave me the bloody nose."

"What did he do?"

Tim's lips tightened, and the mulish expression of stubbornness usually reserved for a plate of brussels sprouts spread over his face. "Don't matter."

"Does. Tell me."

"No."

"Was he calling you names?"

"Some."

"Sticks and stones, Tim."

Although Dean knew as well as anyone that names could hurt.

The boy squirmed again—a sure sign that there was either more to say, or he had to pee.

"What else?" Dean asked.

"He said you—"

Dean waited. Tim bounced.

"I what?"

"Never mind."

"This kid said something about me that you didn't like so you slugged him and got kicked out of school for two days?"

"So did he," Tim muttered.

"I don't need you to defend me, kid. I'm a big boy now, and I don't really care what a Janquist has to say."

"He said you were stupid," Tim blurted.

The cab was silent, broken only by the hum of the tires as they turned onto the gravel road that led to the farm.

Huh, Dean thought, names could *still* hurt.

"Not like I haven't heard that before," he said.

He just hadn't figured his son would have to hear it.

"You're not stupid. You're not!"

"Of course I'm not. Neither are you. The people who use words like that are usually scared that they are."

Tim's face scrunched in thought. "You mean Jeremy's afraid *he's* stupid?"

Dean didn't think Jeremy had the brains to know what stupid was, but he didn't say so.

"Maybe. But I wouldn't bring that up to his face."

"*That* would be stupid."

"Mmm."

"Kids say all sorts of things, Dad."

Dean remembered that very well, and most of what they said wasn't nice. If the public schools weren't equipped to handle kids like Tim, who needed a little extra help to "get it," Dean would have been unable to stifle his daily urge to not send Tim there at all.

"I forgot you had a new principal," Dean ventured.

Tim made a face.

"You don't like her?"

"Why? Do you?"

Way too much, Dean thought.

He'd never gotten over Stella, probably never would. But he'd been able to go for weeks at a time without thinking of her since she wasn't around to remind him of all the things he couldn't forget. Now what was he going to do?

"We went to high school together," Dean said.

"You're that old?"

"What?"

"Ms. O'Connell, she looked old."

She'd looked beautiful to Dean. Sure she'd worn a business suit, but the shade had brought to mind autumn leaves and fields upon fields of pumpkins, a time when she'd just left and he'd been missing her.

Her high heels and sheer stockings only emphasized that her legs went on forever.

Dean blinked. His gutter brain was going

to get him into all sorts of trouble. Thinking about how beautiful his son's principal was—what kind of a father was he?

"Ms. O'Connell isn't old," Dean muttered.

"You didn't date her or anything?"

"What? No."

They hadn't dated officially because they'd had to sneak around.

Her friends had considered him an imbecile, his had thought her a geek. Her mother had glared at him as if he were a coyote loose in the henhouse. And her father...

Stella's father had had big plans for his little girl—ones that didn't include her life being ruined by Dean Luchetti. The man had made that quite clear on the single occasion the two of them had spoken.

So Dean and Stella had spent the summer after graduation lying to their family and friends. The only person who might have noticed Dean's absence would have been his best friend, Brian Riley. But Brian had been too busy falling in love with Dean's sister and doing his level best to make sure she loved him back.

Luckily the two of them were married now, and Dean didn't have to kill him. He *had* beaten the crap out of Brian once he'd learned the truth, which had served to clear the air between them.

Good thing Stella didn't have a brother.

"What kind of lady do you like, Dad?"

"Huh?"

Dean took the turn into the long, rutted gravel lane that led to the Luchetti farm. The pickup bounced along the rough road, nearly tossing Tim into the dashboard. The seat belt yanked him back.

"What kind of lady do you like?" Tim tilted his head, and his hair swung over one eye. "You *do* like ladies."

"Don't be a smart guy."

The boy grinned. He'd lost another tooth. Dean couldn't remember if he'd paid for that one yet or not. Since Tim had caught him shoving cash under his pillow one night, Dean had begun exchanging a dollar for a tooth whenever one fell out. Not much magic in the transaction, but Tim didn't seem to care.

"Man to man, Dad, what kind of lady do you like?"

Dean immediately thought of Stella's dark cap of hair.

"Blond," he blurted.

Her long legs.

"Short."

Her college degree and her white-collar employment record.

"Just a plain, hometown girl."

"'Kay. There's lots of ladies like that around here. How come you never go out?"

"Most of the women in Gainsville know me."

"Then they should love you."

"Not exactly."

"I love you."

Warmth spread through Dean's chest as it did every time Tim said those words. Considering what the kid had been through before coming here, it was a wonder he could love at all.

"Same goes," Dean said. "But I'm not what you'd call a great catch."

"You can catch. Real good."

Dean parked the truck in front of the

main house and turned to look at his son. Tim loved football—would play every minute of every day if Dean let him. He worried about Tim joining the peewee football team this year. The boy was so small.

"Not that kind of catch. I meant, I'm not exactly a fun date, or good husband material."

"Why not?"

"I'm crabby. I have no patience. And I'm a farmer. I'll never be rich."

"You're not crabby, you're funny. You have lots and lots and lots of patience with me. 'Sides, who needs to be rich? We're happy."

Tim threw himself into Dean's arms, and Dean caught the scent of little-boy sweat.

Kid smelled just like sunshine.

CHAPTER THREE

STELLA WALKED INTO the house. Like every other door in town, her parents' was unlocked. The television chattered in the den; dishes clinked in the kitchen. Stella had missed dinner.

A typical occurrence in the life of an administrator. She'd had several meetings with teachers after school, then stayed to look in on cheerleading practice and band rehearsal.

When she'd lived alone, no one had been there to care if she didn't show up by a certain time. Now she'd only hear how foolish she was for trying. Why had she come home again?

Stella set her briefcase and purse on the hall table. Let the canned laughter from the television and the cool breeze from the window wash over her.

Oh, yeah. She'd wanted to find some peace. Foolish to think she could find it here. Even without Dean Luchetti appearing in her office.

"Stella?"

Her father. The man had ears like a bat.

She moved to the doorway. "Hi."

He swirled the soda in his glass, making the ice cubes clink merrily. The merrier the clink, the angrier he was.

Clink, clink, clink.

Uh-oh.

Stella stepped into the room. She might as well get this over with. Then she could escape to a warm bath, good book and even better cup of tea.

"You're late."

"I left a message."

"What kept you?"

"Meeting, meeting, meeting, cheerleading, band."

"Why is it your responsibility to oversee everything?"

Stella turned a snort of laughter into a cough. She patted her chest, cleared her throat and tried to speak with a civil tongue. "Because that's what my responsibility is. You asked me to take this job, Father."

"Take, not obsess over."

Stella shook her head. If she was going to do something, she was going to do it right, not blow off her duties because the school wasn't up to a certain standard.

"I hear there was trouble today," he said.

How did he get information so fast?

Stella sighed. Because this was Gainsville, and everyone knew everything, sometimes even before it happened.

"You expelled the child, I assume?"

"Expelled? Hardly."

"He doesn't belong."

"Janquists have been here since Gainsville was a truck stop."

"I didn't mean him, and you know it."

Clink! Clink! Clink!

She knew.

"Tim Luchetti deserves the same treatment as every other child."

"He isn't a Luchetti."

"He will be."

Her father shot her a quick, annoyed

glance. He'd caught them kissing that one time, but he'd ordered her never to see Dean again and she'd pretended to agree. He'd never mentioned "the incident" again.

Still, she'd often wondered how much he knew about that summer. Couldn't have been much, or Dean would have sported a shotgun-size hole in his chest. Her father might be a card-carrying elitist, but he still kept his granddaddy's shotgun handy in case someone got fresh with his women.

Her father swirled his soda even faster.

Stella had looked at Tim's file after he'd left. Most of the entries were clinical. Notes from Tim's doctor, information about his meds, results of psychological, physical and intelligence testing.

The kid wasn't crazy; he was healthy and really quite smart. Tim needed guidance, stability, two things he appeared to be getting from the Luchettis. With specialized help from the school he'd do fine.

Stella had dealt with a thousand kids who had been diagnosed with ADHD. Schools, especially public schools in large cities, overflowed with students on a variety of medication.

Most ADHD children could be charming—they learned to get along by their wits. Tim was no different.

"Don't go getting any ideas," her father said. "You aren't keeping that dead-end job."

This from the man who'd insisted she take it. Of course, she'd never been able to figure out George O'Connell. Never been able to please him, either, so she'd stopped trying.

"I want that drug baby out of our school system."

"What drug baby?"

"You called him Tim."

"He's not a baby and he's not on drugs."

"His mother was."

"You knew his mother?"

"No."

Stella gritted her teeth and counted to ten. "Maybe you should tell me what you do know."

"There isn't much."

"How unlike you."

Her father was the biggest gossip in town.

He ignored the jibe; maybe he hadn't heard it. Must have had a bad day at the Bank of Gainsville. Perhaps some teller had misplaced ten whole dollars.

"No one knows anything about the child, not even the Luchettis."

"How could that be? Social services should have a file."

"They do, but there's precious little in it. He doesn't even have a name."

"It's Tim."

"He chose that himself. They found him in an alley in Las Vegas."

George's lips pursed at the mention of a place he considered the third ring of hell. What sane person would throw away good money on the turn of a card?

"He was abandoned?" Stella asked.

"So he said. He has no recollection of his parents, or any city before Las Vegas."

"How long was he on the streets?"

"He doesn't remember anything but that."

Stella frowned. Tim was lucky to be alive.

"What about shelters, social services in Nevada?"

"Nothing."

"No one's claimed this child?"

Except Dean.

"No. Who knows what you're getting with a street kid? I hear he's defective."

"He's fine," she snapped.

Her estimation of Dean went up. Adopting a child with ADHD wasn't easy. Adopting a child without a past, giving him a future was downright saintly. She could almost forgive him for breaking her heart.

Almost.

"Explains why the adoption isn't final yet," she murmured.

"Why?"

"No records. They're probably trying to find out who he is and if someone's looking for him."

"What if they do?"

"I'm not sure."

If Tim's mother showed up, or even his father, a court just might turn him over. She couldn't imagine the devastation that would cause the people who loved Tim.

Dean was putting his heart on the line for the good of a child who wasn't even his. Another reason to admire him—not that she needed one.

Stella frowned. She didn't dare fall for Dean Luchetti again.

She'd barely survived the last plunge.

AS THEY DID NEARLY EVERY night, Dean and Tim walked through the cornfield separating their house from his parents'. His mother insisted it was foolish for Dean to make dinner for two at his place and her to make dinner for two at hers. She was used to cooking for an army. Dean wasn't used to cooking at all.

"Do I have a birth certificate?" Tim asked.

He'd been coming up with all sorts of questions this afternoon. Dean had tried to work the snot out of the kid, both in punishment and in an attempt to shut him up, but it was near impossible to wear Tim out. Contrary to popular old wives' tales, exercise didn't curtail hyperactivity—and sugar didn't increase it. Go figure.

"I'm sure you have one."

"You just don't know where it is. Like my real mom and dad."

"Yeah."

"That's why I don't have a birthday."

"You've got a birthday. We just—"

"Don't know when it is. Stinks."

It did. One of the best things about being a kid was having a day that was all yours.

"Why don't you pick one? Until we know any different, and we may never know, any day you like can be your birthday."

"Really?"

"Sure. Why not?"

"Okay. Tomorrow."

"*Tomorrow?* But—"

"What's the matter with it?"

"Nothing," Dean said. "It's just September 11."

"So?"

"You remember we talked about the towers that went down? The planes crashing?"

Tim hadn't been born at that time, so he didn't recall the day, but the footage was shown enough every year for him to "remember" like everyone else.

"Evil, terrorist scum!" Tim shouted.

"Uh, yeah." The kid had been talking to his grampa again. "That was September 11."

Tim stopped walking and looked up at Dean. The sun shone brightly behind his dark head, making a kind of halo. Dean had to smile. The kid was really the cutest thing on two big feet.

"Wouldn't it be good to make that day happier?"

"Not sure we can. What about the next day? September 12?"

"If my birthday was on the bad day, would that make me bad?"

"Of course not. The men who flew those planes were bad. The day has nothing to do with it."

"Then that's my birthday. Nine-eleven." His lips tightened. "I want it."

Nice one, Dean. His dad was going to have a ballistic fit when he found out Tim had picked Patriot Day for his own.

Except Dean's father surprised him.

"Great idea, champ." John ruffled Tim's hair. "Let's have a party."

"A party?" Tim's eyes went wide.

"Why not?"

"Dinner's ready." Eleanor came in from the kitchen. "Why not what?"

"Have a party for Tim's birthday."

"Which is when?"

"I chose tomorrow for my birthday, Gramma. Isn't that the best day?"

Eleanor glanced at Dean and he shrugged. As far as he was concerned, Tim could have a birthday every day. The kid deserved it.

"Sure," his mom said. "I'll bake a cake. We'll have a picnic."

"And presents?" Tim asked.

"What would a birthday be without presents?" She opened her arms. Tim threw his around her ample waist and held on.

Dean was struck again by the odd feeling that aliens had secretly replaced his mother with this woman. In his youth, Eleanor had never been cuddly. She hadn't had the time. She'd loved them all, and they'd known it. But six kids in seven years meant her fuse was shorter than short.

They'd all walked on eggshells around

her for most of their lives. They still did. Since menopause had hit a few years back, her fuse was now nearly nonexistent.

However, to her grandchildren, Eleanor Luchetti was a gentle, loving safety zone in the middle of a scary world.

"What do you want for your birthday, kid?" Dean asked.

Tim released his gramma, then let his bright, excited gaze touch each one of them before he did a dance of excitement and breathed, "A pet pig."

Eleanor groaned and smacked herself in the forehead before returning to the kitchen. The ensuing bang and crash of pots and pans made everyone jump.

Tim glanced at Dean. "Whad I say?"

STELLA FINALLY GOT THROUGH a week at Gainsville Elementary without having to suspend any more pupils.

She'd seen Tim Luchetti from afar. He spent every recess playing some imaginary version of football by himself. He also sat alone at lunch and walked to the bus alone after school. She didn't like that at all.

Stella spoke with his teacher, but after only a week and a half in the classroom, Mrs. Neville didn't feel qualified to make a judgment. Nor did she feel it was necessary to call Tim's home. Except for the fight, which Stella had already handled, Tim was the poster boy for a properly disciplined problem child.

So there was really no reason for Stella to climb in her car and head for the Luchetti farm after school. No reason at all beyond her nagging unease and her annoyingly romantic dreams of Dean Luchetti. She wished she'd never seen his face—both at seventeen and last Monday.

Balloons trailed from the Luchettis' mailbox, an oddity that didn't strike Stella until after she'd started down the long, rutted driveway.

The yard was full of cars. They had company.

She couldn't turn around because the land around the road was too rocky for the low carriage of her rented four-door crapmobile. She had to coast nearly to the house before she could even attempt a

Y-turn. By then, everyone had dropped whatever it was they were doing and gathered on the porch to stare.

Stella had no choice but to get out of the car. As soon as she did, a herd of dogs trapped behind a fence on the far side of the house started barking. One dalmatian and four...who knows what.

"Silence!" Mrs. Luchetti snapped.

Every dog stopped mid-yip. Stella wished she had that power. It would come in handy at assembly.

She recognized everyone on the porch— Dean's mom and dad, his sister, Kim, and Brian Riley.

She frowned. Last she heard, Kim had taken off and not come back, leaving Brian devastated. Then his parents had died in a car accident and he, alone, had inherited the farm.

Brian didn't appear alone any longer if Kim's hand on his shoulder and the adorable little girl in his arms were any indication. The child, attired in a navy-blue star-spangled dress and matching hat, leaned over and began to coo at her ruby red slippers, which was the cutest thing Stella had seen since someone had brought a kitten to school last week.

"Hello." She raised her hand, feeling like a fool. "I didn't know you were having a family get-together. I'll just leave."

She reached for her car door.

"Stella?" Kim asked. "What are you doing here?"

"Here, here? Or Gainsville here?"

"Both."

"Dean didn't tell you?"

Brian frowned, which made Stella nervous. Brian and Dean had been best friends. How much did he know?

Stella straightened, staring Brian right in the eye. If anyone had anything to be embarrassed about it was Dean. She'd loved him; he'd used her.

Brian glanced away, but since the little girl had lunged at her shoes and he'd had to haul her back, Stella wasn't sure if he was guilty or merely busy.

"Ms. O'Connell is the new principal at Gainsville Elementary," Mrs. Luchetti explained.

"Acting principal," Stella corrected. "While they try to replace Mrs. Little."

"Oh, good." Kim shuddered. "Woman still gives me nightmares."

"You and every other kid who ever went near her," Stella said.

"Evening house call by the principal," Dean's mom murmured. "What did Tim do this time?"

"This time?" Stella asked. "Oh, you mean Monday."

"I mean pretty much every day. He's a handful. In my opinion, Mrs. Little wouldn't have made it through the year with Tim around. He'd have worn her out."

Terrific, Stella thought. Just what she needed was Dean Luchetti in her office every day.

She had a sudden flash of him and her kissing and she choked, then began to cough.

"You okay?" Dean's father hurried down the porch steps and smacked Stella on the back hard enough to dislodge a lung.

"Yes. Sorry. The hay. I'm a bit allergic."

"To hay?" Mr. Luchetti said, his expression completely mystified.

"Come on inside, then," his wife ordered. "I'll get you something to drink, and you can tell me what the trouble is."

"I should probably talk to Dean."

Mrs. Luchetti shot her a look that made Stella tremble in her sensible black pumps. Why had she thought it a good idea to wear a gray pin-striped pantsuit to a farm?

"I mean in addition to you, of course," she blurted.

Kim snickered and Brian muttered, "Shh."

"Shh! Shh! Shh!" The little girl put her finger to her lips and made exaggerated shushing sounds, blowing spit all over her hand and her father's neck.

"Thanks, Zsa-Zsa," Brian grumbled, dabbing at the wetness with the collar of his T-shirt.

"Zsa-Zsa?" Stella couldn't help but ask.

"Hi!" The child waved, smacking her father in the eye. Brian merely sighed and toted her toward the swing set in the backyard.

"Her real name's Glory," Kim explained. "But she's got this thing for shoes and hats, glitter and feathers. Always has. Dean started calling her Zsa-Zsa and..." Kim shrugged. "It stuck."

That sounded like Dean.

The thunder of feet could be heard an instant before Tim skidded out the front door. He frowned at Stella. "You weren't invited."

"Tim!" Mrs. Luchetti snapped.

"She wasn't."

"She's come to talk to your father."

"I didn't do it," he said immediately.

"You don't even know what it is yet," his grandmother pointed out.

"I didn't do nothin'."

"He didn't," she assured everyone.

"Stella?"

Dean appeared in the yard. His boots were encrusted with mud, or something far worse. His shirt was sweat-stained, his pants filthy. He was still the most handsome man she'd ever seen.

"I didn't meant to interrupt," she said.

"Doesn't seem fair to have the principal

at my birthday party." Tim kicked at the dirt with a worn tennis shoe.

"Your birthday?" Stella murmured. "I thought—"

"I picked it." Tim glowered. "It's mine now."

"Okay." She glanced at Dean, who spread his hands.

Stella could understand Tim's hostility. What kid would want the principal to attend his birthday party?

"If I could just talk to you for a minute," she said.

"I should clean up." Dean looked down and frowned.

"Not on my account."

The dogs started barking again and everyone glanced toward the road. A brown delivery truck bounced in their direction. Moments later, a blond pixie in an ugly tan uniform hopped out.

"Tim Luchetti?" she asked.

"That was fast," Tim said.

"What did you order?" Dean demanded.

Stella glanced at the boy to see if Dean's tone frightened him, but Tim had scooted over so he was standing directly in front of the delivery woman.

"Mommy?" he asked.

She blinked. "Whoa. Not me, kid. I already got three at home."

Tim turned a forlorn expression toward his father. "But I wished I'd get a mommy for my birthday. And she's exactly the kind of lady you said you wanted, Dad."

Dean rubbed his forehead. "Tim."

"You said blond, short, just a plain girl."

Dean lowered his hand, and his eyes met Stella's. She wasn't so dense that she didn't understand he'd described a woman exactly the opposite of her. Stella glanced away and met the curious, contemplative gaze of Dean's mother. Then she didn't know where to look.

"This is for you."

The delivery woman deposited a box on the ground in front of Tim, then hopped into her truck and left as quickly as she could.

The container shimmied, rattled, and something inside began scratching to get out.

"Oh," Tim said, and smacked himself in

the head. "This is the *other* thing I wished for."

"If that's a pig in there," Mrs. Luchetti announced, "someone's gonna die."

CHAPTER FOUR

"Take a breath, Mom."

Dean inched past Stella, gritting his teeth when he caught a whiff of her perfume. Something light, which made him think of new flowers, fresh grass.

What was she doing here?

Dean didn't have time to find out. From his mother's expression, he needed to move fast or risk an eruption.

"Not a pig." Tim was so excited he could barely stand still. "Nope. But can I have one?"

"Sure. Why not?" Ellie said. "Take a cow, too, while you're at it. Want a sheep?"

Tim glanced from his grandma to Dean. "Is she bein' sarcastic like you said? I can't tell."

"Never mind." Dean reached for the opening on the box as it rattled and shook and growled. He had a sneaking suspicion he knew what was inside. Even if it wasn't a pig, someone was in big trouble. Thankfully that someone wasn't him for a change.

"Wait just one minute." Dean's mom crooked a finger at Tim. "What exactly did your dad say?"

Tim glanced at Dean and he nodded. When Eleanor Luchetti asked a question in that tone of voice, you'd better answer. Actually, when she asked any question at all, at any time, anywhere, answering immediately was the best policy.

"He said you're the queen of sarcasm." Tim's huge feet shuffled, shooting up puffs of dust from the gravel driveway. "Whatever that is. But it's good to be the queen, right?"

His mother's eyes narrowed, and Dean was possessed by the sudden urge to hang his head and confess to everything he'd ever done and several things he hadn't. How did she do that?

"It's always good to be the queen," she agreed, and Dean relaxed. "Now, what's in that box and who do I get to blame for it?"

Tim's smile faded. "Uncle Bobby asked what I wanted."

Bobby. Dean walked around the container until he found the address label from Mexico. He should have known.

Even though Dean's older brother was off only Uncle Sam knew where completing daring Delta Force missions, Bobby kept in contact with Tim through his wife, Jane—a physician currently saving lives in the deepest jungles of Mexico.

"Uncle Bobby's in big trouble," Dean's mom murmured.

"If you can catch him," Kim said.

Since the bad guys were never able to, Dean doubted their mother would have much luck.

Preoccupied with thoughts of Bobby, Dean didn't keep a close enough eye on his son. By the time he noticed Tim tugging on the end of the box, it was too late. A final heave and the thing fell open, revealing an animal containment cage.

"Wait—" Dean said, but he shouldn't have bothered. The instant Tim saw the catch on the door, he flipped it and a bundle of long legs and spotted fur shot out—headed straight for Stella.

Her eyes widened; she stretched out her hands, backing up and shaking her head as she made soft, helpless sounds in the back of her throat. Sounds that caused Dean to remember things he had no business remembering at his son's birthday party.

"No!" Dean's mom shouted.

Unfortunately this dog didn't know her well enough to be properly cowed. Every other animal in the vicinity froze, but not the mutation.

The long, gangly, butt-ugly puppy launched itself at Stella, hitting her in the thighs. She wobbled, pinwheeling her arms, then went over like a house of cards in a high wind.

Dean winced when her rump met the grass, tensed when her head met the earth with a dull thud, started running at the sound of her shriek, which was loud enough to give the impression the dog was tearing out her throat.

He was at her side in an instant, yanking the overly zealous animal off her chest in mid-slobber, then shoving it into the waiting clutches of his father, who banished the beast behind the fence with the rest of them.

"Hey." Dean fell to his knees and helped Stella sit up. "Did he hurt you?"

She was pale, stunned, tousled. Her chin was slick with dog spit. One of her shoes had fallen off. The top button of her suit jacket had popped.

"I—" Absently Stella pulled on her jacket. "I'm not good with dogs."

"I remember."

Her parents had never allowed Stella to have a pet; therefore, anything with feathers or fur had been foreign to the point of fear. She'd always been nervous at the farm, and the only way to calm her down had been to—

His gaze dropped to her mouth, and he had to force himself to turn away.

"Why do they always come right for me?" Stella asked.

"It's a mystery," he said, hauling her to her feet and making the mistake of looking back into her face.

He was captured by the flecks of yellow amid the green of her eyes. How many times had he stared into them?

Her lips trembled. He wanted to kiss her until they stopped.

"You don't like dogs?"

Tim's voice made him start and take his hands off Stella's elbows. How long had he been staring into her eyes, remembering?

Dean glanced around at his family. His dad was dealing with the dogs, along with Brian and Zsa-Zsa. His mom had run into the house—no doubt to fetch her box of Band-Aids, Bactine and Valium.

But Kim was watching him with a speculative expression. Of all his siblings, Dean wanted Kim to know his secret the least.

Though things between them had been better since she'd married his best friend, they'd never gotten along. Which was his fault. He'd been jealous of the princess who'd appeared in their midst when he was two and a half.

Dean was the first to admit he had issues, but lately he'd tried to focus more on his strengths than his weaknesses—

the strengths being farming and sarcasm, a perfect blend of both his father and his mother.

He had never wanted anything other than to work this land, live his life, love this woman.

He had to stop thinking like that.

He'd given Stella up for her own good— broken her heart and his own so she could live the life she was meant to lead. He'd thought he was over her, but even if he'd thought wrong that didn't mean he was going to tell her so. Stella still didn't belong here, and she never would.

Dean stuck out his tongue at Kim. She merely smirked and wiggled her eyebrows.

"I've always been a little scared of dogs."

Stella's voice made him turn away from his sister.

"Scared?" Tim's lip curled in disbelief. "Of a *dog?*"

"Pathetic, isn't it?"

"Yeah."

"Tim," Dean warned.

"She said it first." Tim snorted. "Can I go play with my puppy?"

"It isn't yours yet, kid. You gotta convince Gramma there's room for another mutt on this farm."

"Okay!" Tim skipped off to play with the herd behind the fence.

"Think he can convince her?" Stella asked.

"Oh, yeah. Tim's got Mom wrapped around his finger."

"That doesn't sound like the Eleanor Luchetti we all know and fear."

"I keep telling everyone she's been replaced by a pod person."

Confusion flickered across her face, so he explained.

"*Invasion of the Body Snatchers*. Aliens come to Earth and replace everyone with look-alikes, which come out of pods in their basements."

"Oh, yeah. I remember that movie."

"I checked the basement," Dean continued. "No pods."

Stella gave a short laugh.

"I was serious," Dean muttered. "But no one believes me. They say the grandkids have mellowed her."

"Grandkids do change people."

"So Mom says." Dean frowned at Stella's torn and grass-stained clothes. "I'm really sorry about this. I'll pay for your suit."

"I should have known better than to wear it."

"You've been gone a long time," he said.

"Some things never change."

Dean cast her a quick glance, but she was staring at tiny cow-shaped dots on a faraway hill and not at him. How could fourteen years have passed and she still looked the same? How could she look the same, and be so different?

And she *was* different; he just couldn't put his finger on exactly how.

"What things?" he asked.

Stella started as if she'd forgotten he was there, then shrugged. "Never wear a light-colored suit to a dairy farm."

She smiled, and Dean suddenly understood what had changed. Stella's smile had always lit up everyone and everything around her—certainly him. Stella had great teeth, courtesy of Daddy's money and the only orthodontist in Gainsville.

Dean's were just a little crooked and always would be.

But it wasn't the straightness or the whiteness of her teeth that had made Stella's smile special, or the loveliness of her skin or the green-brown shade of her eyes. What had made Stella's smile light up the world had been the expression of happiness that came from deep within.

Now her mouth faked a happiness no longer found in her eyes. Why was Stella so deep-down sad?

"Is there somewhere we could talk?" she asked.

"We are talking."

"About Tim."

"Privately, you mean?"

"Yes. Although your mother seemed to want to be in on the discussion."

"My mother wants to be in on everything." Dean headed toward the cornfield, stopping when Stella didn't follow. "You coming?"

She eyed the waving stalks. "Don't tell me your office is down row five. I've heard that one before."

His lips tilted at the memory. Moonlight on the cornfield. Him and her in the center kissing, surrounded, shielded by the six-foot-high plants.

Dean's memories brought a wave of regret, and because of that, he growled. "I live in the thresher's cottage now. You wanna talk private, we do it there."

He strode into the field. If she followed fine; if not, fine, too.

STELLA PLUNGED INTO the field, following the slightly waving stalks, which revealed Dean's path. By the time he popped out on the other side, she was right behind him.

The cabin had been built aeons ago to house threshers. In times past, a threshing machine was too expensive for everyone to own, so it had moved from farm to farm, and the owners of the land provided housing and food for the workers, along with modest pay.

Stella shook her head. She was remembering trivia in an attempt to forget her memories. She wasn't going to be able to remain in town very long at this rate. Everywhere she went she was assaulted with memories of them together.

Dean climbed the porch steps and opened the screen door. Stella hung back.

"You don't want to come in?" he asked.

His eyes were open, curious, holding none of the memories that had to haunt hers. How could he forget that they'd met here, too? How could he live in this house? How could he breathe?

Stella forced herself to take air in through her nose, then let it out through her mouth. A little trick she'd learned her first year of teaching—not only did it calm panic attacks but prevented fainting and hyperventilating.

In a few seconds her heart slowed. She gave herself a quick talking to. If Dean could forget, so could she.

Stella lifted her chin, stomped up the steps and preceded him inside. One glance and she felt better. Everything had changed.

Back then, no one had lived here, which was why they'd come. The floors had been dirty, the windows cracked, the walls streaked. Bats had lived in the ceilings and mice in the corners. That she'd spent any time in the place at all only proved how much she'd loved Dean.

The cottage was now completely redone—new floors, windows and drywall, paint, curtains and furniture. Soft footballs, T-shirts and socks were scattered around. Dirty dishes littered the countertop.

Her throat got a little thick at the sight. The place no longer looked abandoned; it looked like a home. So very different from her apartment in L.A., where everything was white, not a speck of color there or in her life. The apartment wasn't home— never had been, never would be.

Where were these strange thoughts coming from? She'd liked her life just fine— until it changed.

"Sit." Dean swept out a hand, indicating the living room. "You want anything?"

For an instant her gaze flicked to the smooth, tanned hollow of his throat. He swallowed, and her stomach danced.

"No." She moved out of the hall and took a seat on the edge of the sofa. "Thank you."

Her voice was cool, remote. Principal

O'Connell was back. Stella felt so much better.

Dean sat in a chair that was as far away from her as he could get and still be in the same room.

She cleared her throat. "About Tim—"

"He told me he's been behaving. Was that an exaggeration?"

"No."

"Then why are you here?"

"I'm worried about him."

"What did he do?"

"Nothing."

Dean was silent for several seconds, then shrugged. "You lost me."

"He seems lonely."

Dean's lips tilted upward. "Ain't we all?"

Stella frowned. How could he be lonely in the middle of such a huge, loud, loving family? Dean had a son, probably a girlfriend—or ten. She doubted the local women had sworn off him for good, especially once they'd gotten out in the world and discovered that while Dean might be sarcastic and short-tempered on occasion, he was a good man at heart, and those were very hard to find.

"Tim's a kid," she said. "He should have friends."

"He's got friends."

"Really? I've never seen him with anyone."

Dean scowled. "He hasn't been in school that long."

"*How* long?"

"Since last year."

"A boy should make friends more quickly than that, Dean," she said quietly.

"I never made friends very easily, either." He shrugged. "I had no patience, even at six."

"You had your brothers and Brian. You didn't need anyone else."

Not even her.

"I was a lot like Tim," Dean continued, glancing at his hands, which were clenched between his knees. "I couldn't sit still. Did a lot of dumb stuff."

"You weren't dumb," she said automatically, the way she'd always said it whenever her friends had called him that.

"I know." He lifted his gaze. "I was *just* like Tim."

The light dawned. Why hadn't she seen it before?

"ADHD," she said, and Dean nodded.

She'd already been beyond impressed that Dean had taken on a child with the disorder, but knowing he had the same problem sent her estimation of him even higher. In truth, he was probably the best man for the job of raising Tim since he knew firsthand what the child was going through.

"When did you find out?"

"Last year. Tim bamboozled me into taking the tests with him. I think he was scared, though he'd never let you know it."

"No wonder," she murmured.

"No wonder what?"

"You had a hard time focusing. You couldn't sit still. You never paid attention."

"I was a problem child."

"You couldn't help it."

"I could. I just didn't want to."

"You didn't want to because it was more difficult for you than everyone else, and back then no one knew what to do, except label you difficult and stick you in shop class."

"I liked shop."

As an educator, Stella should have recognized his condition before she was slapped in the face with it. Of course, she hadn't been an educator then, and now...now she wasn't sure what she was anymore.

"No one knew much about ADHD until the late seventies and early eighties, and in a small town like this, it was even later," she said. "It's a wonder you made it through school at all."

He shrugged. "Didn't really matter since I never wanted to do anything but farm."

Which also made sense. Farmers spent a lot of time outdoors in the wide-open spaces. They spent very little of their life sitting still. Being successful was based on common sense and hard work, which wasn't a bad way to gauge success, come to think of it.

Not that sufferers of ADHD were stupid. Quite the opposite. They were often very intelligent, but unable to focus their attention for a reasonable amount of time.

Age, practice and, in some cases, medication helped.

"I can't force Tim to make friends," Dean said.

"Maybe he could join a club or a sport. Something that would get him involved with children from the area."

"After last week, I'm not all that enthralled with the children from the area."

"They aren't all like Jeremy Janquist."

"Good thing. Tim has had enough rough stuff in his life."

"What kind of rough stuff?"

"He was abandoned. Smacked around. I haven't been able to get all the details out of him. It's a miracle he can function at all, that he can trust, that he can even sleep at night. I consider myself lucky he isn't a budding serial killer."

Stella winced. She'd seen enough of those already.

"There's no record of his family, or him, anywhere?" she asked.

Dean cast her a quick glance. "You've been reading the file."

She'd been listening to her father, but she wasn't going to tell him that.

"What does his having no records mean for you and Tim and the adoption?"

"Things are moving, but slowly. I have temporary custody. Aaron and his wife, Nicole, have been helping me since they know a lot of people in social services."

"What if someone else claims Tim?" she asked.

Dean clenched his hands, and an expression of such desolation washed over his face she almost reached out.

"I'll fight for him," he said. "His parents dumped Tim somewhere alone, and they never came back. They didn't want him, but I do. I won't let him go."

Stella had never known Dean to be this certain of anything, except farming, which only proved she didn't really know him at all.

She was finding his responsible, loving side as attractive as his muscley, hard-working side, and that meant trouble. She'd only embarrass herself if she started drooling and he noticed. Being turned down by the man once in her life was quite enough, thank you.

"I'm thinking Boy Scouts would be good for Tim," she blurted. "Maybe 4-H?"

"He wants to play football."

She shuddered. "At seven?"

"Eight. Today."

"Oh." She recalled the balloons. "Right. How did he discover his birth date?"

"He picked one."

"Why today?"

"He said he wanted to make the day happier."

"Good luck," she muttered.

"Yeah." Dean tilted his head. "You don't have a problem with his making up a birthday? Usually administrative types get their knickers in a twist about stuff like that."

"I've got better things to twist my knickers."

Silence followed her statement and she swallowed. That had sounded suggestive. Just about everything did when she was around Dean.

His gaze dropped to her left hand. "You aren't married?"

"No," she said shortly.

He lifted his eyes. "Were you?"

"No."

The air between them seemed to hum with all the things they'd said and quite a few they hadn't.

Stella sighed. "I came about Tim."

"I didn't figure you came for me. You left me behind a long time ago."

Her eyes widened.

He saw her expression, then stood and strode to the window. "I don't know how we're going to do this," he said.

"What?"

Her voice had gone breathy. From the sudden tension in his shoulders, he'd noticed.

"Live in the same town. Stand in the same places where we once—" He made an impatient noise deep in his throat. "You know. I can't pretend we were never together, Stella, even if I'm supposed to."

"I didn't think you remembered."

He stared out the window. In the distance, the sound of childish laughter was punctuated by a symphony of barking dogs. Adults shouted. Cows lowed. Life went on.

So why did it seem as if they were right back at the beginning?

"I remember everything," he murmured. "All the time."

CHAPTER FIVE

STELLA'S STARTLED GASP affected Dean like a soft punch to the gut. He never should have said that.

"Dean, I—"

He spun around. "You what?"

"I don't know. Nothing's really changed. I'm not staying, and you won't leave, right?"

"Right."

There'd be ice in Satan's backyard before he left Gainsville for anything other than a vacation. Not that he ever took a vacation, but whatever.

"You didn't love me."

He'd said that to make her go. So she'd have the life she'd dreamed of. The life she could have, should have, without him.

He'd lied, but he couldn't tell her that.

What good would it do? They'd only get their hearts broken again when she left.

The devil on his shoulder whispered: *Why not date again?*

But Dean was no good at dating, never had been. Besides, he had the kid to think about now. Tim wanted a mom. He deserved one. Dean wasn't exactly sure how he'd get him one, but he wouldn't start by dating his son's principal for the few weeks or even months she was in town.

In Gainsville everyone knew everyone else's business, and sooner or later everyone would know that. How mortifying. For him, for her, but especially for Tim.

Dean couldn't do it.

He considered it a miracle they'd managed to keep what had happened between them fourteen years ago from becoming common knowledge.

Stella never would have been able to live in his world, no matter how much he might have wanted her to. She would have wilted and died here—or at least their love would have.

He'd been right to make her go. She'd

have wound up resenting him, hating him, and that he couldn't bear. Although she didn't appear to like him too much right now, and she wasn't going to like him any better in a few seconds.

Well, better a clean break than a slow, ugly death. The same rule applied today as it had fourteen years ago.

"I didn't love you," he said. "I'm sorry."

He watched her face, which had once been so expressive. He'd been able to tell every shift in her mood by that face. He couldn't any longer.

"Don't be," she said. "You can't help who you love, or who you don't."

She stood and turned away.

"No," he murmured, letting his gaze wander over the long, slim line of her back. "I can't."

"I should let you get back to the party."

"I'll walk you over."

"You don't have to."

"That's where the party is."

"Oh. Right. Duh."

She headed straight out the front door,

across the porch, and then the yard. Dean had to hurry to catch up.

"Why are you here?" he asked.

"To talk about Tim."

"I didn't mean *here,* here. I meant in Gainsville. You haven't been to town in fourteen years, Stella. Why now?"

She seemed to shrink in on herself, though she made no movement beyond walking, ever forward and away.

"I think Tim will be fine," she said. "We shouldn't have to see each other, unless I run into you inadvertently."

She'd completely ignored his question, and her words made him forget what he'd asked.

"What are you talking about?"

"I know you don't want to see me any more than I want to see you."

"I didn't say that."

Stella stopped at the edge of the cornfield and turned. "You said you couldn't look at the places we'd been together and not remember." She stared into his face. "Why do you remember? I'd have thought you forgot me the instant I walked out of your life forever."

"Not forever. You're back."

"But I won't be for long."

A warning—as if he'd needed another.

"Don't *you* remember?" he asked.

Something flickered in her eyes, but he wasn't sure if it was anger or pain. Why did he keep picking at this sore?

He couldn't help himself. This was the first time he'd felt alive since she'd left.

"I didn't," she said. "Until I came here."

She plunged into the cornfield, almost immediately disappearing from view amid the thick stalks. Dean hurried after.

"Nostalgia is a powerful thing," she said. *Nostalgia.* Was that what this was?

"The first kiss is important to a woman," Stella continued. "We never forget."

For some reason, her answer bugged him. As if it didn't matter who her first kiss was with, just that it was the first.

"What about the hundred kisses after that?" he demanded.

"Some of those I forgot." Stella glanced at him and sighed. "Relax, Dean. You were the stud of Gainsville. Every kiss is a gilded memory I've never let go. There's never been another man like you. There never will be. Feel better?"

Not really.

When had she become so angry, so brittle? Was it because of what he'd done? Or was it something else?

Stella reached the other side of the cornfield and burst into the front yard, leaving Dean behind. He stood still, trying to figure out what he'd done besides tell the truth—or at least what she thought was the truth. Then he caught sight of her heading for the car and he ran.

Thankfully his family was nowhere to be seen, because he really didn't want them to see this.

She got into the car, slammed the door, forgot to shut the window, started the engine. He reached in and switched it off.

She smacked his hand. "Who do you think you are?"

Anger flashed in her eyes. At last, a hint of the old Stella.

"What are you smiling about?" she snapped. "You look like a goon."

He hadn't realized he was smiling, but since he was, he smiled wider. "I wondered where you'd gone."

"To L.A. Your attention span hasn't improved."

"Why did you leave there and come back here?"

The anger fled. The mask returned.

Aha, he thought. *Something happened in L.A.*

"I don't know what you mean." She reached for the key again.

He clamped a hand on her arm and she flipped out.

Maybe *flipped* wasn't the right word because she didn't thrash, or scream or slug him. Instead she froze, fear darkened her eyes and she started to breathe in tiny, terrified gasps.

"Stop," she whispered.

Dean withdrew his hand, but he continued to lean into the window. Stella had always been the most confident person he knew. She hadn't been the prettiest girl, but she'd been the smartest, the most interesting, the nicest—at least to him.

Now she seemed lost, unsure, frightened—of what he couldn't quite figure, because she couldn't be frightened of him.

Could she?

"What's the matter?" he asked.

"I—I—" She took a deep, shuddering breath. "I don't like to be grabbed. Especially in a closed place where I can't get away."

"Since when?"

She just shook her head and reached for the key again. He made an involuntary movement to stop her and she flinched.

"Hey," he murmured. "I'd never hurt you."

She gave him a dirty look.

"I mean physically."

"I know." The stark pools of her eyes made him want to take her into his arms and hold her tightly until the fear went away.

"What happened in L.A.?"

Her lips trembled, and for a second Dean thought she might tell him. Then a shriek from the house made him jump, and he banged his head on the roof of her car. Muttering, he straightened and turned.

The new puppy shot out the screen door, followed by Tim, then Dean's mother. She had a spatula in her raised hand.

With his attention elsewhere, Stella started the car. Dean swung back, but she'd closed the window, probably locked the doors. Hitting the gas, she spun gravel and disappeared in a cloud of dust down the lane that led to the highway.

STELLA STOPPED THE CAR when she was out of sight of the Luchetti farm. She couldn't drive much farther with her eyes tearing and her chest aching.

She was such a wimp.

How was she ever going to return to L.A. and the job she loved, the job she was good at, if she fell apart every time someone grabbed her arm?

And that wasn't the only thing that sent her over the edge. If she was startled when she was alone, or if anyone taller and stronger than her got too close, if someone made a fast, unexpected move in her direction, Stella dissolved into a frightened, stuttering fool.

But she hadn't thought she'd be frightened of Dean. That she had been for just an instant only proved she wasn't getting better, she was getting worse.

Stella leaned her forehead on the steering wheel and strove for calm. What if she was never able to go back to working with high school kids? What would she do with the rest of her life?

"I'll find something," she said.

But what?

Concerned that a local police cruiser might stop to see what was the matter—they didn't have much else to do—Stella forced herself to put the car into gear and drive home. Then she sat in front of her parents' house and tried to think of somewhere she could go. She didn't want to talk to either one of them about anything, especially this.

Her family didn't know why she'd come back. No one did, and she wanted to keep it that way.

Since she had nowhere to be, no one to visit—all of her high school honor roll pals had fled Gainsville and *they* hadn't returned—Stella dragged herself out of the car and into the house.

"Stella?" her mother called from the kitchen.

A quick glance into the den revealed her father wasn't home, thankfully. The rush of relief made her wonder if renting an apartment while she was here might not be a bad idea. Living with her parents was upping her stress level higher than a riot in the cafeteria.

"Hey, Mom." Stella stopped in the doorway. "Where's Dad?"

"Work."

"This late?"

Carrie O'Connell shrugged. "He can't seem to catch up on his paperwork."

"Oh." Her father had never stayed late or gone into the office on Saturdays when she was a child. But the world had changed, and probably banking had, too. Though you'd think with the advent of computers there'd be less paperwork rather than more.

"Where did you go?" her mother asked.

"The Luchetti farm."

Her mother's eyebrows shot up. "Why?"

"A problem with one of the kids."

"I didn't realize any of the Luchettis had children old enough to be in school."

Carrie had never kept up with the intricacies of Gainsville as Stella's father had. She spent a lot of time in the garden. She knitted layettes, which she donated to a home for single mothers in Chicago. She took care of the house, shopped, made meals and, every so often, played bridge.

Stella had been as desperate to escape a repeat of her mother's life as she'd been to escape Gainsville itself.

"Dean's adopted—or rather adopting—a little boy, and he attends Gainsville Elementary."

"Dean?" Her mother's eyes widened. "Isn't there someone else at the school who can deal with him?"

"It's my job, and, anyway, why would I do that?"

"Your father and Dean—" She shook her head. "They don't get along."

"Still?"

"He had no business kissing you."

Stella flashed on the earlier scene in Dean's yard, when he'd touched her and she'd gone nuts. She doubted he'd be kissing her again. Which was a good thing.

So why did she feel so bad?

Then she realized her mother wasn't talking about today—how could she be?—but rather fourteen years ago.

"He had every business kissing me, Mom. I wanted him to."

Boy, she still did. Her freak-out that afternoon notwithstanding.

"You really shouldn't get involved with him again, dear. Your father's heart isn't good. Upsetting him now like you upset him then—"

"I'm thirty-two years old, Mom. I'll see who I want, when I want."

Although it wasn't going to be Dean, but she didn't have to tell her mother that.

"Your father isn't going to stand for that man coming around here."

Stella thought about the conversation she and Dean had just had.

I didn't love you. I'm sorry.

Why did that hurt as much now as it had then? She'd moved on. Or at least she'd thought she had until she'd moved back, seen him, remembered everything.

"Stella?"

"Don't worry, Mom. I doubt Dean Luchetti will ever come here again."

"Daddy!"

Tim's shout kept Dean from jumping into his pickup and chasing after Stella.

Something had happened in L.A. to make Stella return to Gainsville—something that had made her eyes sad, her manner beyond nervous. He didn't care for any of the scenarios he was imagining. He also didn't care for the rush of anger that warred with a feeling of helplessness. She'd been hurt, and there was not one thing he could do about it.

Tim threw his arms around Dean's waist, then climbed his body like a monkey until he had a stranglehold on Dean's neck.

"She's going to kill Rodgers."

Dean's gaze met his mother's as she lowered the kitchen utensil. "Mom, what did we say about the *K*-word?"

She scowled. "The little monster ate the birthday cake right off the table!"

Dean peered at Tim. "Why would you do that?"

Tim rolled his eyes. "Not me. Rodgers."

"I take it Rodgers is the name of the new puppy."

Tim looked sheepish. "Is it okay if I name him after Aaron Rodgers?"

Dean winced. "Do you have to?"

Rodgers had beaten the Bears so many times it was embarrassing. Thankfully, he was now retired.

"I guess I could call him Cubby. Like the Cubs. Then he'd fit in, right?"

Dean glanced at the scraggly, spotted hound, which had brains enough to hide behind the pigpen. He doubted his mother would chase the beast there.

Then again, it depended how mad she was.

"I'm not sure he'll fit in anywhere, kid, but he does seem more like a Cubby than a Rodgers."

Tim peered at the dog, which gave a low *woof* then ducked behind the building when Eleanor glanced his way.

"I guess," Tim said.

Something sticky slid down Dean's cheek and he wiped it off.

Frosting. Tim seemed to have quite a bit in his hair.

"Maybe you should give Cubby a bath, and yourself, too, while you're at it."

"'Kay." Tim wiggled until Dean set him down. The kid ran off to corral the dog, and Dean was left to deal with his mother.

"Whoops?" he said.

She smacked him in the forehead with the spatula.

"Hey! What was that for? I didn't get him a dog."

"Bobby's not here. What *did* you get him?"

"I'm taking him to Bloomington to buy football cleats."

"Football?"

She glanced at the dog and the boy, who appeared to be using the hose to create a pig wallow. They were going to be covered in mud by the time they finished washing off the frosting. To give her credit, his mom didn't bat an eye. Eleanor Luchetti had dealt with bigger messes than that every day of her life.

"Do you think football's a good idea, Dean?"

"He wants to play."

"You wanted to fly, as I recall, but that didn't mean I let you jump off the barn roof."

"I just did it when you weren't looking."

The spatula twitched as her eyes narrowed. "I'm finding out way more than I ever wanted to know now that you guys think you can talk to me like adults." She tilted her head, and her heavy, white braid swayed. "Did you fly?"

"Sure. Until I fell. I think I broke a rib."

"And why did I never hear about this?"

"You'd have popped a blood vessel." Dean shrugged. "Why beg for trouble?"

"I want to go back to the days when you hid things from me."

"Really?"

"No. Tim's too little for football."

"He's quick and he's tough."

"So he's going to outrun the Neanderthals?"

"That's the theory."

"I don't like it. And I don't like that mutt. I walked in and found the beast buried to its eyeballs in chocolate cake."

"We could send him back. Let Tim have a pig instead. I don't think a pig could climb onto the kitchen table."

"You are so funny. Ha-ha. I'm going to bust a gut laughing."

"I thought you'd like that."

"Fine. He can keep the puppy, but make sure it stays out of my way."

Eleanor stalked back into the house. Dean glanced at Tim, who was as wet and muddy as his new pet. The kid was staring at him with a forlorn expression that turned to utter joy when Dean gave him the thumbs-up.

Tim began to dance in the mud, and Dean's chest tightened. He'd never thought he could love again after Stella. Then Tim had shown up and everything had changed—including Dean. He wanted to be a dad. He wanted to have a family, a home, a life. Loving Tim had started to make Dean wonder if he could love another woman besides Stella.

Dean glanced down the road. Now he wasn't so sure.

CHAPTER SIX

"THIS WAS THE BEST DAY ever." Tim threw his arms around Dean and clung.

"I'm glad."

His dad sat on the side of Tim's bed. Tim had taken a real bath. The one with the hose hadn't worked so good. Both he and Cubby had ended up messier than when they'd started. Stuff like that happened to him a lot.

But now he was scrubbed with soap—head to toe—and Cubby was, too. Tim would never admit it, but he liked bein' all fresh and clean and tucked into bed by his dad.

No matter how long he hugged Dean, Dean never pulled away first. That was one of the nicest things about him. It was almost as if he understood Tim needed to be

the one to let go. Knowing Dean, he probably did.

Tim released his dad's neck. Dean ruffled Tim's damp hair with his big, hard
hand. Tim loved those hands. They were
so wide and rough and strong. They could
hurt, but they never, ever did.

"Can Cubby sleep with me?"

"Not until he knows better than to pee
on the bed."

"He wouldn't."

"Yes," his dad said, "he would."

When Dean spoke like that, Tim gave
up while he was ahead.

"Gramma said he could stay, right?"

"Right. Just keep him out of her way."

"That ain't gonna happen."

"I know."

"Sunday are we goin' to Bloomington to
get my shoes? You gonna call the football
coach and see if I can play on the team?"

"You bet."

Tim smiled. His dad hadn't broken a
promise yet.

There was still one thing about today

that bothered Tim, and he wouldn't be able to sleep if he didn't ask.

"What did Ms. O'Connell want?"

His dad hesitated, and Tim held his breath, trying to remember what he'd done that might make the principal come to his house. But he hadn't done nothin'.

Lately.

"She said you don't have any friends."

"Is that weird?" Tim's voice trembled, and he bit his lip, then glanced at his dad to see if he'd noticed.

He had. Dean always noticed stuff like that.

"I never had friends, either." He tweaked Tim's nose. "And weird is only weird if you let yourself think you're weird. Does that make sense?"

"No."

"What *you* think about yourself is what matters."

Tim squinted at Dean through his bangs. "Were you ever *in* second grade?"

Dean laughed and brushed Tim's hair out of his eyes. "I know it seems like what other people think is important, but it really isn't. I guess I didn't learn that until I was out of school."

"You didn't need no friends," Tim said, "you had the uncles."

"True."

"I need brothers."

Dean sighed and Tim felt kind of bad about complainin'. His dad was doing the best that he could.

"Even if I got married tomorrow," Dean said, "had a baby next year, by the time he, or she, was old enough to be any fun, you'd be too old to care. I think you're going to have to make some non-Luchetti friends, Tim."

"I don't wanna."

"Tough tootsies."

Tim giggled. Now that his dad had stopped swearing, he was starting to make up all sorts of goofy words to take the place of the curses.

"Lights out now, okay?" Dean leaned over and kissed Tim's head.

Dean might be big and strong—a manly man he said, and then made He-Man noises and flexed his muscles—but Dean always kissed Tim good-night, and goodbye and good morning, as well as a few more in between. And Dean never turned out the lights until Tim told him it was okay.

"'Kay," Tim said, and the room went dark.

For some reason his dad thought he should be scared of the dark, but Tim never had been. Sure, bad things happened in the night, on the street, when you were all alone. But those days were gone. Besides, he'd always promised himself that if he ever had a place to live, if he ever found a family, he'd never have to be afraid of the dark again.

And he wasn't.

Tim loved falling asleep to the sounds of his dad watching TV, or doin' the dishes, or just movin' around. When Tim heard those noises he knew he was home, that he wasn't alone, and fallin' asleep was easy.

Once they'd moved to the cottage, Tim had even stopped creeping into Dean's room in the middle of the night. He'd stopped sleeping at the foot of Dean's bed, trying to make sure Dean wouldn't disappear like every other adult in Tim's life.

Before he'd met Dean, Tim had figured he was unlovable. Sure he was cute, which was why people took him in. But once they knew him, they always threw him out. Except for the Luchettis.

Gramma Ellie said once you were a Luchetti every other Luchetti loved you forever no matter what. Just look at Dean. He was the biggest pain in her behind since a horse had kicked her when she was five, and she loved him to pieces.

Gramma always punctuated this statement with hugs, kisses and tickles so that Tim knew she loved him, too, and always would.

Until today, he wasn't sure if he'd really believed that. But when Cubby had eaten the cake, then tracked chocolate all over the floor, and Gramma had yelled and chased them, she hadn't caught them and she could have.

Gramma might say she was old, but she was quick, and Tim knew it.

He'd been yelled at, chased and threatened with the spatula.

Tim was definitely a Luchetti now.

AFTER DEAN HAD CLEANED the kitchen and watched the news, he sat on the porch and fleetingly wished he still smoked. He wouldn't subject Tim's lungs to the second-hand fumes, nor risk getting cancer and leaving Tim without a dad.

Unease came over him. Life was iffy at best. There were a lot of ways to die on a farm. Heavy machinery fell on people all the time. Bulls got loose. Haymows collapsed.

If those things weren't enough—Dean's gaze flicked over the impossibly flat land—tornadoes were as common as corn. He needed to get that adoption put through and fast. He had to make certain that if Tim didn't have him, he'd always have someone. Luchettis stuck together; they took care of their own.

The sound of tires on gravel drifted from the road. Dean recognized Brian Riley's green pickup truck even before it got close enough to see a color. He'd been expecting him.

Brian greeted Dean with a nod, then tossed a soda can into his lap and popped the top on his own. He set the other four cans on the porch between them and took the remaining chair.

"Gonna be an early winter," Brian observed.

"Who says?"

"Farmer's Almanac." Brian took a long pull from his soda. "Usually right."

Dean grunted and opened his can. Then he waited. Brian only came over these days with a good reason.

For years Brian had been as alone as Dean. They'd spent their twenties becoming the farmers they'd always dreamed of being. Then Kim had returned, and Brian had lost his mind.

Not that Dean wasn't glad his sister and his best friend were married. But Kim had broken Brian's heart, and Dean had been the one left behind to pick up the pieces. It hadn't been pretty.

Luckily worrying about Brian had helped

Dean get over his own shattered love life. Although, now that Stella was back, Dean realized he'd never gotten over her at all.

Brian drained his soda and popped another. Must be a serious problem.

"You still have a thing for her," Brian said.

Slowly Dean lifted his can, drank, then lowered it. "Who?"

Brian merely took another sip and didn't bother to answer.

Dean sighed. "You knew?"

"Always."

"Kim?"

"I think she's suspicious now, but not then."

"*How* did you know?" Dean asked.

"You were happy."

Dean, who had lifted the soda halfway to his mouth, lowered it. "What?"

"Face it, Dean, you were never a jolly fellow." Brian toasted him and drank. "But that summer you smiled too much."

"That's a crime?"

"Not a crime, but a concern. Add to the overabundance of grinning the fact that you disappeared a lot, then came back with straw in your hair, dust on your pants—"

"Maybe I was working."

"Is that what you called it?"

"I loved her," Dean snapped, then wished he hadn't when Brian's eyes went shrewd.

"Really? I always wondered what happened. Why she left, why you let her."

"Why do you think? She didn't belong here any more than Kim did."

Brian winced. *Oops.* Still a sore spot. Dean could hardly blame him. Kim had wanted nothing more than to get out of Gainsville. Not even Brian's love could keep her down on the farm.

"Kim didn't belong here then," Dean hastened to add. "But she does now."

"Exactly. And maybe Stella does, too."

Dean frowned. "Huh?"

"Things change and so do people."

"Not Stella. You saw her. She's allergic to hay for crying out loud. She's afraid of dogs. She wore a suit and heels to a dairy farm."

"Kim used to do that."

"Just to be annoying."

Brian grinned. "She *is* cute in heels. I kind of miss them."

"Spare me."

"You still love her," Brian accused.

Dean had been contemplating the cornfield, but at that he turned his head in Brian's direction. "It shows?"

"Big time."

"Son of a cock-a-doodle-do."

Brian choked mid-swig and sprayed soda all over the porch. "Sorry, but your cuss words are killing me."

Dean rubbed his forehead. "Do you think she knows?"

"That you love her? I'm thinking no, since she took off this afternoon like she was never coming back. What was that all about?"

Dean wasn't going to share with Brian his theory that Stella had been hurt in L.A.—it was only a theory—so he improvised.

"I told her I never loved her."

Brian's eyes widened. "I take it back— you really are as dumb as you look."

"Stella and I—we— It wouldn't work."

"You haven't tried."

"She was never meant for this place, man. She always wanted something more."

"She wanted you."

"She wouldn't have for long. She'd have wound up hating me as much as she hated Gainsville. Things aren't any different now. She isn't going to stay. I can't go."

"You sure about that?" Brian asked.

"That she's going? Yes."

"That you have to stay."

"I don't think there are too many dairy farms in L.A. Besides, I don't care if I'm alone for the rest of my life, Tim isn't living in a big town ever again."

"You're right." Brian nodded slowly. "Tim belongs here."

"And I belong with Tim."

"Impasse. Unless you told her the truth."

"Which is?"

"That she's the woman you've been waiting for all of your life."

Dean considered throwing the remainder of his soda into Brian's face, but he hated to waste it. "You're a moron."

"I know." Brian grinned. "Why don't you go talk to her?"

"Now?"

"Sure. I'll stay with Tim."

Dean wanted to talk to Stella, but not to tell her he loved her. *He* wasn't a moron. He wanted to ask about L.A.

Dean stood and tossed his empty can over his shoulder, smiling when Brian caught it. Then he climbed into his truck and traveled the still-familiar path to Stella's house.

THE DAY HAD BEEN as dull as Stella remembered. Nothing to do but read or watch TV. Stella suggested a movie, but her mother wasn't interested in seeing anything that was showing at the Gainsville Duplex, and neither was Stella.

Stella's father had never come home, which was worrisome, though her mother didn't seem upset. In fact, she'd seemed kind of glad.

Her parents' marriage had always been one of polite disinterest. Stella had never understood why they'd stayed together.

Of course, divorce in Gainsville was rarely done. The divorce of the bank president and school board member—not happening.

Stella's mother had very few options if she left. She'd gone to college but received a degree in art history. She'd never had a job. Carrie was better off living in her house, working her garden, pretending everything was fine and being taken care of in the manner to which she was accustomed.

Just because Stella wanted to shriek and bang her head against the door didn't mean her mother felt the same way. In fact, her mother didn't seem to feel much at all. Stella was starting to wonder if she was heavily medicated.

No doubt her parents' lack of affection, to her and to each other, as well as the overly polite state of their marriage, was what had drawn her to Dean in the first place. He'd been so alive, so passionate, so different.

Every man she'd dated since had been the complete opposite of him, which might explain why she'd been bored out of her skull by them.

Stella went to bed early—tired in mind, but not body—hoping that the next day would be better than the last. But first she had to get through the night, and that proved a lot more difficult than she'd expected.

Stella had a dream—a long, dark, heart-pounding terror of a dream. She came awake with a gasp, blinking at the room of her childhood, believing for an instant that she'd retreated to a place of safety in her mind, even though her body still resided in her apartment in L.A.—or maybe a nearby psych ward.

Then she heard the distant chug of a train and understood she was in Gainsville, and for the first time since she'd returned, she was glad.

A quick glance at the clock and Stella groaned. The dream had seemed to go on and on, yet she'd only been asleep for half an hour. Now she was sweaty, shaky and wide-awake.

Stella climbed out of bed, changed her

nightgown and washed her face, then headed downstairs. Hesitating on the landing, she listened to make sure no one else was awake. She did not want to talk right now.

The house was silent, still. However, what should have been peaceful was, in the wake of her dream, creeping her out. The place was stifling, so she moved toward the front door, grabbing her mother's sweater and wrapping it around her long, white granny nightgown.

Quietly, Stella shut the front door, then stood on the porch, uncertain. The psychiatrist she'd seen in L.A. had recommended meditation for stress relief, and she'd tried, really she had. But each time Stella tried to clear her head, her mind rebelled, instead filling with every thought she'd pushed away, her brain roiling like a lake beneath a thunderstorm.

She descended the steps and moved into the middle of the yard, enjoying the sensation of cool grass against her hot feet, a light breeze stirring her damp hair. Throwing back her head, she stared at the sky.

One thing about farm country, the heavens were clear, the stars and the moon almost painfully bright. In L.A. she couldn't remember the last time she'd been able to see more than the faded twinkle of a handful of stars pulsing dully beyond the smog.

Out of the corner of her eye, Stella caught the sparkle of the moon off the hood of a vehicle parked in her father's space on the far side of a storage building. She didn't give it a second thought, momentarily consumed with joy that she wouldn't have to worry he'd show up and ruin her new mood.

Staring at the sky, breathing in and out, listening to the silence, she started to experience the sense of peace the psychiatrist had promised. Her pulse slowed; her chest eased; the pain in her shoulders melted away.

Slowly Stella lowered her gaze from the indigo sky. She turned, and her heart gave a solid, painful leap. A man lurked in the shadows.

Her gasp split the night. Her dream had come alive. She wasn't sure if she should scream or run. She discovered she could do neither. She began to tremble and she hated herself.

"Stella?"

Dean's voice.

The shadow separated from the night, stepping into the silver glow of the moon.

Dean's face.

She was so relieved, she got dizzy with it. So dizzy, she had to sit. Right on the ground.

"Hey!" He hurried across the grass, dropped to his knees next to her. "You sick?"

She shook her head, only realizing that tears marred her cheeks when they flew free at the movement. Taking a breath, she was horrified to hear a hitch in the middle, as if she'd been crying for hours.

"That's it," Dean growled. "You're telling me what happened in L.A., and you're telling me now."

"N-nothing happened."

Nothing she was going to tell him, anyway. He might have been closer to her than anyone on the planet fourteen years ago, but those days were gone along with part of her sanity.

Dean reached out slowly, as if he understood that fast moves scared her. Cupping her chin, he tilted her face. The wind cooled her tears; the light of the moon glistened off the tips of her damp eyelashes.

Dean used his thumbs to wipe the last droplets from her cheeks. Their gazes held; the awareness that had always been between them hovered. His eyes lowered to her lips, and for an instant she thought he might kiss her. For an instant she wanted him to.

Until she came to her senses.

Kissing Dean would lead to nothing—she couldn't start dating the father of one of her students. Wouldn't that look spectacular on her employment record?

Besides, Dean had broken her heart once, she didn't think she could survive his breaking it again. She was in bad enough shape as it was.

But there was one thing she was in desperate need of.

"I could really use…"

"Hmm?" Dean leaned forward, his breath brushing her lips, promising things he'd always delivered.

"A friend," she said.

"A friend?" He inched back, dropping his hands from her face.

"Yes."

Stella held her breath, hoping Dean would agree. He didn't love her, had never loved her, and that hurt. But he had always made her laugh. He'd made her live. When she'd hung out with Dean, she'd been happy, and she wanted to be happy again.

Dean glanced away, staring at his truck parked in her father's spot. Then he gave a short, sharp laugh and glanced back.

"Sure," he said. "I'd like to be your friend."

DEAN COULDN'T BELIEVE he'd agreed to be Stella's friend. Whenever he came near her, all he could think about was how good it had felt to hold her, to be held by her.

But he could see that she needed a friend. So much more than she needed a boyfriend.

Maybe being her friend would help him get over her. Remembering what they'd shared, dreaming of the scent of her hair certainly wasn't working.

"Why me?" he blurted.

"What?"

"Why do you want me for a friend? I'm sure you've got plenty."

She gave a sad smile. He really didn't care for that smile, but he had no idea how to get the other one back.

"None of my friends from high school are here anymore."

"Oh, right. But what about L.A.?"

"They aren't there, either."

Duh.

"Tell me what happened there," he demanded.

She started again and he wanted to smack something, but that would only scare her more.

"Why do you think something happened?" she asked.

"Stella, you had nerves of steel when we were kids, and considering your old man, that's saying a lot."

"What are you talking about?"

He shouldn't have brought up her father. That was dangerous territory.

"Your father scared everyone, except you. With a dad like him I'd have thought you'd be a nervous, skinny bird child."

She glanced at the house. "Like my mother."

"I didn't say that."

Although now that she had... Her mother was so quiet and ghostly, sometimes he forgot she had one.

"You never let your dad push you around." Dean let his head fall back as he gazed at the sky. "I admired you for it."

She didn't answer, and he lowered his gaze to hers.

"I'm not like that anymore," she whispered.

"You let him push you around now? He must love it."

"Amazingly, no." At Dean's confused expression, she continued. "He asked me to take Mrs. Little's job, yet when I did, he wasn't happy. He called me a nose wiper."

Dean's fingers curled into fists. Her dad was still a jerk. Imagine that?

"Let's forget about him and get back to L.A."

"I wish I could," she said wistfully.

Dean contemplated Stella. She appeared so young in that white nightgown. Like Wendy from *Peter Pan*.

"What happened?" he asked again.

"I'm fine." She looked away.

"I never said you weren't. But something happened there, Stella. Something that made you run back here, and that means it was pretty bad."

Her eyes met his, and Dean knew she wasn't going to tell him—friend or not. Maybe she couldn't.

As a "friend" he shouldn't push it, even though he wanted to. When she was ready, she'd tell him, or at least he hoped she would. For now, he'd move slowly, talk quietly, let her heal and try not to go mad wondering what, or who, had hurt her.

"Maybe you shouldn't be working," he said.

She straightened as if someone had

goosed her. "If I can't do this job, I'll never be able to go back to my old one. I will *not* let anything or anyone take away the most important thing in my life."

The most important thing in her life was her job. Why did that bother him so much? It wasn't as if there was a chance in a million she'd say the most important thing in her life was him. He'd made sure she'd never say that again.

However, Dean understood why her eyes no longer laughed. If farming had been taken from him, he didn't know what he'd do.

"I'm sorry, Stella. I wish I could help."

She took his hand. The gesture was so natural, at first he didn't even notice she'd done it. When he did, he was merely glad.

How was he ever going to be her friend when he loved her so much?

"You're very sweet," she murmured. "I never noticed before."

"*Sweet* is not a word usually applied to me. Ask anyone."

Without realizing it, Dean had begun to run his thumb over her palm. Her hands were slim, white and soft, while his were big, dark and rough. The contrast made his stomach flutter.

When had they inched closer? *Who* had inched closer? Him? Her? Did it matter? He turned his head, and she was so close her breath mingled with his.

"Dean," she whispered, and the years fell away.

The kiss was light, gentle, a mere brush of lips, nevertheless his heart thundered so fast his chest ached.

But so far the kiss could be passed off as a friendly peck; anything more would be decidedly unfriendly. Dean lifted his mouth from hers.

Her eyes were closed, her face pale and still, as if she were savoring the moment, committing it to memory forever. She reminded him of a sleeping princess from one of Zsa-Zsa's movies, and he was possessed by the insane desire to be the man who awakened Stella from her spell-cast sleep.

Dean leaned in closer and he caught the scent of apple trees in autumn. He feathered

his lips over her closed eyelids, pressed a
single kiss to her forehead, then worked his
way from her cheeks to her chin. She shuddered, her hands clutching his shoulders,
pulling him closer, not holding him away.

His mouth hovered over hers. Her eyes
slowly opened.

Then headlights washed over the yard,
freezing Dean and Stella in mid-embrace.

CHAPTER SEVEN

STELLA SCRAMBLED TO HER feet, feeling once again as if she were seventeen and caught kissing a boy by Daddy. From the expression on her father's face, he remembered.

Dean stepped in front of her; she shoved in front of him. Her father shut off his car and threw open the driver's-side door.

"What are you doing?" he shouted.

Stella wasn't sure which one of them he was talking to. Probably both. Nevertheless, she spoke first. "None of your business."

Dean slid an uh-oh glance her way, but he kept quiet. Good choice. Anything Dean said right now would only make things worse.

George O'Connell's mouth opened and shut like a fish thrown on the banks of a lake. "What did you say?"

"You heard me. I'm thirty-two years old. I can do what I want."

"You're not taking up with that half-wit again."

"Half-wit?" Fury spread through her with such force her hands shook. "He's got a higher IQ than you do."

"What?" Dean blurted.

Stella shrugged. "I peeked in the files."

"Bad girl," he said, but he smiled.

"What have you got against Dean?" Stella demanded.

Her father's lip curled. "Besides the manure under his fingernails?"

Dean frowned at his hands, which were perfectly clean.

Stella sighed. "Never mind. You never could see past the nose on your face."

"I didn't have to look far to find him."

"We—" Dean began, but Stella gave him an elbow in the stomach so that he said "oof," instead.

She'd walk a block in south central L.A. in the middle of the night before she'd let her father know that she and Dean had agreed to be nothing more than friends.

"Stella," her father said, "you can do so much better."

"'Better' is in the eye of the beholder."

His lips tightened. "You aren't going to take up with Luchetti under my roof."

"We weren't under your roof."

Her father's face flushed. She needed to stop baiting him before he had a stroke, right on the lawn.

"Let me put it this way," he said. "I see him again, you find a new place to live."

Stella shrugged. "Fine by me."

"Stella—"

Dean stopped speaking when she narrowed her eyes.

Her father appeared shocked. Had he actually thought that threat would work? She'd been living alone for ten years. She had enough money even without the Gainsville Elementary principal's job to rent an apartment.

Unless…

"You want me to vacate the job, too?" Stella held her breath.

Amazingly, she didn't want to lose the job, and she wasn't sure why. Maybe because she didn't want to fail at one thing so soon after failing at another.

"Of course not," her father blustered. "I'd never do that."

"There is no one else," Dean muttered.

He was probably right.

"Well," Stella said when no one else spoke, "good night, Father. It's been fun. I'll find a place to rent tomorrow."

He hesitated as if he meant to say something, then made a disgusted sound and stomped toward the house. "Get your truck out of my parking space," he growled as he passed Dean.

Instead of making his usual sarcastic rejoinder, Dean stared at Stella with a frown as her dad slammed the front door. "You've been thrown out of the house because of me."

"I never should have stayed here in the first place," Stella said. "I probably never should have come home."

"No," Dean said, and brushed her fingers with his. "I'm glad you did."

She did feel better than she had in months, but that was probably just the adrenaline high from telling her father to go away. Or maybe her euphoria was merely the result of the hormones that had leaped for the first time in years at the touch of Dean's mouth on hers.

Either way, she felt good. The nightmare had been returned to the dark where it belonged. Sooner or later she'd have to confront what frightened her, talk about it with someone other than her psychiatrist, but not now.

"Why didn't you tell your father we're just friends?"

"I didn't want to."

Dean laughed. "You're getting as bull-headed as me."

"Impossible."

Stella contemplated Dean's face as she asked the next question, one that had been gnawing at her for years. "What did you say back then to make him dislike you so much?"

"I think his feelings had more to do with what I was *doing*."

"Oh!" Stella fought not to blush and lost,

so she went for flippant. "Well, no harm, no foul. It was just a simple kiss."

Dean's forehead creased.

"Not that it was bad!" Stella blurted.

"Your father thought it was."

"It was long ago. So what's up with him now?"

Dean tossed his keys into the air, snatched them before they fell to the ground, then turned away. "I can't imagine."

DEAN DIDN'T HAVE TO imagine. He knew exactly what was wrong with Stella's dad.

When O'Connell had threatened to have Dean arrested for trespassing fourteen years ago, Dean had told him to get lost. Other than that, Dean had no idea why they weren't the best of friends.

He waved at Stella as he wheeled out of her dad's precious parking space. He had to admit, he'd parked there on purpose. Maybe that was why George wanted to strangle him. Dean couldn't resist needling him whenever the opportunity arose.

Not that it arose very often. The two of

them had avoided each other ever since Stella had gone away.

He reached the cottage in minutes. Brian was still on the porch, and there were three sodas left.

"What have you been doing?" Dean asked.

"You're lookin' at it." Brian stared at the sky and breathed in and out as if he were practicing yoga.

Dean frowned "You okay?"

"Yep. Sometimes I just need a little space, you know?"

"You were desperate with loneliness because the princess left you, and now that she's back, you need space?"

Brian lowered his gaze to Dean's. "You got a problem with that?"

"Not me. I'm the one who wanted her to move to Kazakhstan."

"You talk big, but you love her."

"Goes without saying." He glared at Brian. "And I mean, *without* saying."

Brian shook his head. Being an only child, Brian had never understood the intricacies of the Luchetti family. Dean and

Kim traded barbs, pretending to loathe each other, but she was still his little sister, and no one messed with her. Not even his best friend.

Kim and Evan, being the youngest, had stuck together against all the others. Colin and Bobby, the middle children, were bound by strife, even before Colin had married Bobby's girl behind his back. That had gotten ugly. Dean snarled at all of them; Aaron attempted to make peace.

They were Luchettis. That was the way things were done.

But Brian wasn't a Luchetti, and he never would be.

"You and the princess lawyer got a problem?"

"What do you care?" Brian muttered.

"Don't be a jerk."

"According to your sister, that's exactly what I am."

"What did you do?"

Brian glared. "Who said *I* did something? You're supposed to be *my* best friend."

"Okay, what did *she* do?"

"Nothing."

"Then why are you at my house instead of home with her?"

"She told me to get lost."

"I doubt she meant forever."

"She doesn't want another baby."

Dean frowned. "That doesn't sound like Kim."

"Are you gonna listen to my problem or keep flapping your yap?" Dean lifted his hands in surrender, and Brian sighed. "Sorry. It's not that she doesn't want one, she doesn't want one now."

"She did just finish law school."

Brian shot him an evil glare and Dean shut up again.

"She wants to wait a year, get her practice going. Maybe even two years, so Zsa-Zsa will be in school."

Dean kept silent until Brian snapped, "Well, don't you have an opinion on that?"

"Am I supposed to?"

Brian did more yoga breathing. "I'd like to know what you think."

"No, you wouldn't."

Because, for a change, Dean agreed with

Kim. Kids weren't easy, and Zsa-Zsa was hard. Besides, Kim had been waiting forever to be a lawyer. Having a baby now would be taking a giant step sideways.

"I'd like to know," Brian said quietly. "Please."

Dean gave in. "I'm just wondering, what's the rush?"

"We lost so much time when she was gone."

That wasn't all they'd lost. The baby no one but Brian and Kim had known about at the time had died before she was even born. Dean couldn't imagine what that had been like for the two of them—losing a child when they were still children themselves.

"Kim just frustrates me sometimes," Brian muttered.

"You, me and very soon the entire legal system. It's her gift. She's a lot like our mom."

"The idea of your mother being let loose on all those innocent lawyers…" Brian gave an exaggerated shiver.

"Yeah, but are there really any innocent lawyers?"

Brian laughed. "Don't let Kim hear you say that."

"Do I seem like I've lost my marbles?"

They were silent for a few minutes, during which the familiar and comforting sounds of the farm washed over them. Sometimes Dean got up in the middle of the night and came out here just to listen. He loved this place.

"You're right," Brian murmured. "We've got time. It's just that she left and I wondered…"

"If she ever really loved you at all?"

Brian's eyes filled with surprise.

"I'm not as dumb as I look," Dean said.

"You never were."

In lieu of a hug, Dean socked Brian in the arm. "She loves you, man. And when a Luchetti loves, they love for a lifetime."

"Really?" Brian rubbed his shoulder. "So what happened with Stella?"

Dean scowled. Trust Brian to get to the heart of the matter. He might talk slow and move the same, but he wasn't dumb, either, and he never had been.

"We're going to be friends."

Brian leaned back in his chair and stared at the stars again. "Sure you are."

TIM WOKE UP AT 5:00 A.M. on Sunday, excited about his day with his dad. Dean was always off on Sunday because that was the day Grampa ran the milking machines.

At the Luchetti farm they had robots to do the work. Well, not robots like in *Star Wars*. But robotic milking stuff and junk. Because of the "bells and whistles" as Grampa called them, only one guy had to supervise the cows getting milked instead of a whole bunch of guys havin' to help.

Tim crawled out of bed, got dressed and tiptoed out of the house, stopping in the living room to let Cubby out of his crate. Then after a quick trip to the outdoor potty, for both of them, Tim skipped through the cornfield with the dog at his heels. He always kept Grampa company on Sundays.

Tim didn't find John in the warm, dark cow barn or the bright, shiny milking parlor. Instead, after trolling through the hay, a little manure, the chicken coop and the near pasture where the sheep were all clustered together like…sheep, Tim found him in the pigpen.

"Hey, kiddo, I was wondering when you'd get here."

"Cubby was in the crate all night, and he didn't go all over himself."

"'Course not. Animals don't mess where they sleep."

"Babies do."

"Baby people. Animals are smarter than that."

Grampa liked animals—a lot—and he knew more about them than anyone.

"So where you been, champ?"

"Couldn't find you. Whatcha doin'?"

"This sow had a litter, but the runt isn't doing very well."

Tim leaned over the fence but not too far. He'd learned the hard way to stay away from the big pigs. Once, he'd shoved his hand through the bars and gotten bit.

Gramma had said, "Well, I told you not to stick your hand in there."

Gramma was like that.

Cubby put his head through the fence, and the sow snorted all over his face. Cubby sneezed and tried to back away so fast he got his head caught. Tim helped him out and saw his grampa watching them.

"It's his first week. He doesn't know."

So far, Cubby had narrowly missed being kicked by both a ewe and a cow, then he'd been pecked by a hen when he pushed his curious nose into her nest.

"He'll learn," Grampa said. "Probably the hard way."

Tim nodded. For him it was always the hard way, which was why he had so many bruises.

He crept closer to the fence. The pigs fascinated him. Always had. They seemed smarter than a lot of the other animals, and Grampa said that was true. Pigs had more brains than sheep, but then what didn't?

"What do ya do with a runt?" he asked.

John lifted one teeny, spotted piglet into his big, hard, gentle hands and watched as it squirmed and squealed, much more weakly than the others.

"Usually get rid of runts." Grampa shook his head. "This one got stepped on a few times."

"How do you get rid of 'em?"

Grampa cast a quick glance his way and Tim knew. Farm life wasn't easy, and while the animals were their life, there was still a lot of death.

"No," Tim whispered.

"He's too small to compete with the others for food. It's only a matter of time."

Tim's lip wobbled, and he bit it to make it stop. "You think that's what happened to me? I was too small, so they got rid of the runt?"

"People aren't pigs, Tim."

"I know, but I'm puny."

"So was I at your age."

"Really?" Tim let his gaze travel all the way up his grampa's six-foot-plus body.

"Yep."

"What happened?"

"I ate right, exercised and did all my homework."

Tim blew a derisive breath from his lips, which made his bangs flutter upward, then settle back down. "Homework don't have anything to do with it."

"Wanna tell your gramma that?"

"Nope."

The two of them shared a smile. They both loved Gramma Ellie to pieces, but she was…a problem sometimes.

"Did you ever read *Charlotte's Web?*" Tim asked.

His teacher had just started reading the book to the class this week. Staring at the piglet in Grampa's hands, Tim figured that was a sign or somethin'.

"Can't say as I have."

"Well, Wilbur, the pig in that book, was small, but he was special."

Grampa John smiled and ruffled Tim's hair with one hand, while continuing to hold the piglet in the other. "Like you?"

"Maybe."

Grampa went silent for a long time; he was thinkin' serious thoughts. "You did say you wanted a pig."

Tim squinted doubtfully. Gramma had said someone would die if that happened.

Of course, she said stuff like that all the time and, so far, not a single death.

"Yes, sir."

"I didn't get you anything for your birthday."

"You got me a Lego train."

Grampa rolled his eyes. "I didn't get that."

Tim grinned. "I know."

John thrust the pig at him. "Go nuts, kid."

DEAN AWOKE AT 4:00 A.M. as he always did, but realizing it was Sunday, he'd rolled over and slept until 6:00 a.m.

He couldn't believe he'd slept until noon and beyond when he was a teenager. He'd missed the best time of the day that way.

Sunrise over the cornfield. The air fresh and new. If it had rained, the droplets would rest on blades of grass, heavy and quivering in the breeze.

Dean got up and leaned out the open window of his bedroom. A cow lowed from the pasture, the sound familiar and soothing. A dog barked and was answered by far too many others.

Now that he thought about it, Dean had forgotten to bring Bear and the doodles back to his place for the night. He was lucky his mother hadn't deposited them on his bed before sunrise.

He hadn't slept as well as he usually did, tormented with images of what *might* have happened to Stella in L.A. How long was she going to keep her secret? How long would he let her?

"As long as it takes," he said under his breath.

She was so twitchy he didn't dare raise his voice or make any fast moves. Not that such behavior would gain her confidence, anyway.

No, what he had to do was be her friend, as she'd asked. When she trusted him enough, she'd tell him, and who knows, maybe in being her friend, he might actually get over her.

"And pigs will fly."

Dean headed for the bathroom. Glancing into Tim's room on the way, he smiled. His son would be helping his father with the chores. Tim was so much like him sometimes it was uncanny. They didn't share blood, but they shared a love of the farm and the animals that would bond them when other things pulled them apart.

Even when Dean and his father had fought, argued, disagreed, they'd still had the farm to bring them together. He hoped the same would be said for him and Tim. Although what he really hoped was that Tim never slid into the awkward and snotty teen years and began to talk back to Dean the way that Dean had talked back to his dad. But he figured that was a vain hope, especially since he recalled quite vividly his dad wishing Dean would have "a son just like you."

"Thanks, Dad," Dean muttered, but he was smiling.

Now that he was past the miserable days of his youth, Dean remembered a lot of great things about having John Luchetti as a dad. He had always allowed Dean to follow him around, John's big hands over Dean's smaller ones as he'd shown him how to attach a milking apparatus to an udder. His father's strong arms wrapped around him as he'd let Dean sit on his lap and steer the tractor, his calm voice explaining the intricacies of machinery, of planting, of farm animals. Dean had lived a charmed childhood on this farm, and he intended to give Tim the same.

A half an hour later Dean was showered, dressed and walking into his parents' kitchen. Sunday morning meant breakfast by Eleanor.

His dad and Tim were already sitting at the table. Dean caught sight of the dogs through the window, lazing in a patch of sunlight. Except for Cubby. He appeared to be chasing something small and not very furry.

Dean craned his head. What was that?

"Hey, Dad?"

Tim bounced so high Dean had to reach out and grab him before he tumbled off the chair.

"Shh," John whispered, and glanced at Ellie while Tim grinned.

Dean frowned. What were they up to?

"You forgot the dogs again," his mother said, not bothering to look away from the stove.

"Sorry."

Ellie flipped a pancake, stirred the scrambled eggs and slid some bacon onto a stack of paper towels. His dad used to eat like this all the time. But since his heart attack, Sunday was the only day of eggs and bacon.

Dean's mom turned, and her eyes widened. Her mouth moved, but nothing came out.

For an instant Dean worried that *she* was having a heart attack, then he saw her gaze was fixed on the screen door that led to the porch.

Posed on the other side of the screen, heads tilted exactly the same way, were Tim's new puppy and, if Dean wasn't mistaken, considering his dad's "shh" and his son's grin, Tim's new pig.

CHAPTER EIGHT

"Grampa said—"

"Hold it right there." Dean's mom reached for her spatula.

Tim's eyes went wide, and he shook his head, refusing to say any more.

"Put down the kitchen utensil," John said. "I told the boy he could have a pig."

"Have, as in fatten for the freezer?"

"Not Wilbur!" Tim exclaimed.

"Oh, no. No!" His mother pointed the spatula at the table, including all three males in her demand. "There will be no naming of the barnyard animals. Once you name them, they just don't make good dinner."

"I think that's the idea, Ellie. I also think it's too late to stop it."

"You did this," she accused.

His dad shrugged, and Dean stifled a

grin. All of his life his mother had blustered and shouted and bossed everyone around, including her husband. John had pretended to let her—then gone along and done whatever he pleased. He rarely raised his voice; he rarely got mad—except at Dean—and his laconic personality was the perfect foil to his wife's borderline hysteria.

"Wilbur's a runt, Gramma. He needs me to feed him or he'll *die*." Tim grabbed his chest and collapsed in his chair with dramatic effect.

Ellie's lips twitched. "I suppose we can't have that."

Tim bounced up. "I'll take care of him. You won't have to."

"You got that right." She glared at John, Dean and Tim in turn. "Let's lay a few ground rules. The pig stays in the pen with all the other pigs. There will be no petlike behavior. No walking on a leash, no sleeping on the porch. Got that?"

"Yes, ma'am," Tim said solemnly.

"This is not *Green Acres,*" Ellie muttered as she turned back to the stove.

"Could have fooled me," Dean said, but she ignored him.

"It's green here," Tim said. "And there are lots of acres. Is she bein' sarcastic again?"

"Yeah."

Tim tilted his head. "I don't get it."

Dean wasn't in the mood to explain the old Eddie Albert and Eva Gabor show, which had been one of his childhood favorites. He'd started to call his niece Zsa-Zsa because of it. So what if he couldn't tell the difference between the two Gabor sisters? Sue him. Glory looked more like a Zsa-Zsa, anyway, and what was funny about the name Eva?

"Eat," Dean ordered in an attempt to distract Tim.

A plateful of food did the trick. If Tim ever caught up to his appetite and his feet, there was no telling how much he might grow.

"We're off to Bloomington," Dean said when the table had been cleared.

"Football cleats!" Tim's chair tumbled

over, a victim of his enthusiasm, hitting the floor with a sharp crack.

Ellie didn't even flinch. She just reached down and picked it up. "Put that pig back in the pen before you go."

Tim, who'd been halfway to the kitchen door, froze. He hung his head and his hair covered his face. "I can't go, Dad."

Confused, Dean glanced at his mother, who shrugged.

"Wilbur's gotta be fed."

"What are you going to do about him when you're in school?"

Tim lifted his gaze. "Maybe they'll let me come home and feed him."

"Nice try," Dean said. "No."

Tim's chin dipped toward his chest, and his sigh was the saddest thing in three counties. Dean glanced at his dad just as his dad glanced at him. They both opened their mouths, but Ellie spoke first. "I'll feed him when you're gone."

"You will?" Tim asked.

"You will?" Dean said at the same time.

His dad just snorted and walked out the door.

"It's not like I have anything else to do." She lifted her brows.

"But you do, Gramma. You do a lot. You cook and clean and wash and—" Tim stopped, and a slow smile spread across his face. "Oh. Sarcasm. I get it."

"Go on." Ellie made a shooing motion with her hands. "The sooner you go the sooner you're back and I'm off pig-sitting duty."

Tim banged through the screen door. Dean's gaze met his mother's. "Thanks," he said.

"Don't mention it."

"Definitely a pod person," he mumbled as he followed his son outside.

"I heard that!" his mother shouted after him.

"You always do."

STELLA AWOKE EARLY. Despite her lack of sleep she wasn't tired. She felt as if she'd come out of a fog. Today she'd take the first step to reclaiming her life. She snatched the paper from the front porch and drove into town, parking in front of the coffee shop.

When she'd left Gainsville, no one would have dared open a place where all they sold was coffee, tea and an occasional muffin. What use could there be for an establishment where people lazed away a morning doing nothing more than reading or talking on their cell phones as they sipped from hand-thrown ceramic mugs?

Obviously someone had found a use, since the homey dining room, complete with a stone fireplace and matching northwoods decor, was nearly full of patrons.

Stella ordered a latte and a bran muffin, marveling that she could do so in the hometown she'd always considered one step short of prehistoric. The information age seemed to have pushed progress everywhere—if you called a coffee shop progress.

Stella took a sip of her latte. She definitely did.

However, the opportunities for shortterm rental were dismal. Guess progress hadn't invaded every aspect of the town, although really, what purpose could there be for apartments to rent by the month in a place where folks stayed for generations?

Stella used to find that quirk beyond annoying. She and her friends often referred to Gainsville as "the town that life forgot." But as time passed, she had discovered that, for most, having your parents, your grandparents, sometimes even your great-grandparents, still living nearby wasn't such a bad thing. It created a sense of continuity, of loyalty to the community, which was reflected in everything around them.

In big cities, the opposite was true. People moved around so much, they had no ties, neighbors didn't form bonds, no one lived near their relatives. In some places, the process of busing inner-city kids to the suburbs ensured that there was no allegiance to local schools or the town.

The residents of Gainsville loved the land and one another. No one went hungry here. No one lived on the street. No one went unemployed for long. They took care of their own, and the idea of "their own" went beyond those of their blood to include anyone within the city limits. So, it wasn't long before Stella had an offer of the perfect place to live—one that hadn't been advertised.

"There's an apartment upstairs," the owner of the coffee shop said after Stella confided the reason for her litany of sighs.

Linda Diangelo was the former vice president of a trucking company in Chicago. After a nasty divorce from her husband, Linda had packed up her only son and relocated to Gainsville.

Linda and Stella had met when Linda marched into school the second day and demanded to meet the woman in charge. Linda had shaken Stella's hand and said, "Do your job and I'll do mine. We'll get along great."

Stella liked that in a parent. She also liked Linda's son, Kane, who hadn't been in the principal's office once.

"You'll just rent me the place like that?" Stella snapped her fingers.

"You're good enough to rule the school, but not to rent an apartment over my coffee shop?"

"Well, when you put it like that…" Stella grinned. "Lead the way."

The two women tramped up the outside staircase. Linda was a bottle blonde, with a pretty face and a lot of curves. What single men there were in Gainsville—around here, they didn't last long—had no doubt been knocking at Linda's door since she'd arrived.

Stella wondered if Dean had been one of them.

None of her business, she reminded herself. She and Dean were "just friends."

"You know the Luchettis?" Stella blurted as Linda opened the door.

Not locked. What else was new? Still, she was glad to see the door *had* a lock. Now, if Linda only remembered where she'd put the key.

"Everyone knows the Luchettis." Linda stepped inside. "They're like the first family of Gainsville."

Stella glanced around. The rental was spacious, extending from the coffee shop in the front, over an empty store in the back.

"You own the entire building?" Stella asked.

"Uh-huh. I might put something in that other store, if I can ever figure out what else Gainsville might need."

"You seem to have fit in here."

Linda smiled. "It's weird. I left to get away from my psycho husband. I figured I'd be bored but safe. But I like it in Gainsville. This place is home in a way Chicago never was."

Stella nodded. She hadn't wanted to stay. However, nowhere else had ever been quite the same.

"Take a look around," Linda offered. "There's a bedroom, kitchen, living, bath. Comes furnished, obviously."

The place had been redone not long ago and was plain, but clean. The furniture wasn't to Stella's taste, leaning toward wall samplers, wicker end tables and plaid sofas, but she could live with it.

"Why were you asking about the Luchettis?" Linda asked. "You must have known them."

"I did. But I was wondering about Tim. Dean's son?"

"Not yet," Linda said.

Stella frowned. "What does that mean?"

"Hey—" Linda held up her hands "—don't growl at me. I was just repeating what I heard."

"Which is?"

"Kid's a problem. ADHD. Fighting. A lot of folks in town don't like it."

"They need to get over it. Compared to some places I've been, and some kids I've seen, Tim Luchetti is easy street."

"I hear you. I remember a few of the nut cakes in Kane's school. And they didn't even have a disorder. They were just screwed up by their families. Too much money, not enough time. The ailment of guilty parents everywhere."

"Is that why you came here?"

"In addition to escaping the crazy husband, yes. I wanted to be around for Kane more than I had been." A flicker of sadness passed over her face. "Once, when I was Ms. VP, he got hurt at school and told his teacher to call his dad, because his mom was busy being important." Linda shook her head. "Of course, his dad was busy being a jerk, but what can you do?"

Stella stifled any comment. She'd learned long ago not to react when parents played the finger-pointing game. "You like owning a coffee shop?"

"I didn't at first. I missed my job in Chicago."

Stella could understand that.

"But it would have killed me eventually. All that pressure. I felt like a mouse on a wheel. Once I got used to the pace here, I started to see that everything's important. Even a little coffee shop in Gainsville, Illinois."

A month ago, Stella wouldn't have agreed. A month ago she wouldn't have understood what Linda was talking about.

How could a coffee shop be as important as a VP position? How could a tiny elementary school in the middle of a great big empty be as stimulating as a huge high school in L.A.?

But a lot of Stella's ideas were changing. She took a stroll around the apartment.

The place would be perfect for her. Walking distance from the school. The coffee shop closed at five, long before she usually got home. There'd be no loud music at night, and Linda didn't open until seven on the weekends. Stella was wide-awake way before that—always had been.

"I think I'd like to live here," Stella said.

"I think I'd like you to."

"Today okay?"

Linda lifted an eyebrow, but she didn't ask what the hurry was. If she'd ever met George O'Connell, she knew.

Linda held out her hand. "Today would be great."

As Stella shook on the deal, she knew it would be.

TIM CLUTCHED HIS BRAND-NEW football cleats to his chest. Shiny and black with a white swoosh sign on the side, they were the coolest shoes ever.

Back when he'd been living in alleys and eating out of garbage cans he hadn't had a hope of playing football. He hadn't even known what football was.

Then he'd come to Gainsville, and he'd found out what he'd been missing. Every Sunday they watched the Bears. Gramma made snacks. Tim got to drink soda. Everyone yelled at the TV. His dad let Tim sit on his lap, and he explained every play. When it wasn't football season, life just wasn't the same.

His dad slowed the truck and wheeled into a small parking lot between two buildings on Main Street.

"What's this place?" Tim asked.

"Pet store. Cubby needs a collar."

Tim followed Dean inside. While his dad peered at dog collars, putting choice after choice back on the shelf muttering, "Too small. Too big. Too poodley." Tim wandered off. He went up one aisle, then down another. He saw every kind of flea and tick shampoo there was in the world.

And then he saw her. His new mom.

He'd kind of forgotten about the mommy quest with all the excitement from his birthday, the dog and the pig. But when he saw the lady behind the counter, Tim remembered.

She was perfect.

She was blond and short. Except for the ring in her nose, she could be a hometown girl.

The lady turned and saw him hovering in the aisle. Her scowl confused him. Until he bounced too much, talked too much, broke something, ladies liked Tim. He was cute and little. Cuddly.

Tim glanced at the floor, dug the toe of his sneaker into the nonexistent dirt, then peered up at her from between his too long bangs and smiled.

Nothin'.

"You aren't supposed to be in here alone."

"My dad's back there." Tim jerked his thumb over his shoulder.

"Don't touch anything. Don't tease the dogs in the cage. Don't pick up the kittens out of the pen."

"'Kay." Tim hadn't planned to.

He wasn't sure if he should ask her about being his mom. That hadn't gone too well the last time he'd tried it with the delivery lady. In fact, when he'd asked guys if they wanted to be his dad, they'd always acted real weird, backing up and sometimes even running away.

Except for Dean. Dean had said yes.

Eventually.

Before Tim could decide what to say to the lady to get her to marry his dad, her eyes lifted, and she smiled for the first time since Tim had seen her.

Tim craned his neck. Dean was behind him.

Maybe Tim didn't have to say nothin' at all.

But his dad just tossed the collar on the counter and reached for his wallet. Sometimes he was so lame.

"Hello," the lady said.

"Yeah."

Tim stifled a groan.

"I've seen you around before."

"Uh."

Tim smacked himself in the forehead.

"I'm kind of new in town," she continued. "What's your name?"

Dean glanced at her, and Tim's heart

stuttered. *Here we go,* he thought. *Just one look and—bam—they'll fall in love.*

"What difference does my name make?" Dean growled.

Tim moaned and his dad put a hand on his shoulder. "Almost done, kid."

"This your boy? What a sweetie!"

Tim beamed. That was more like it.

Dean paid for the collar and grabbed the bag. He started for the door, and Tim had to do something.

"You wanna go out with him?" Tim blurted.

Dean froze, half in and half out the door. His fingers clenched the bag and it made a loud crackling noise in the sudden silence.

"Sure." The lady popped her gum. "When?"

"What time do you get off?"

Dean's glare would have frightened a lesser child. But glares didn't mean nothin'. It was the fists you had to watch out for, and Dean would never use his anywhere near Tim.

Besides, he was doing the right thing. They needed someone to take care of them.

"I'm off at five-thirty." The lady smiled. "You wanna have dinner?"

Dean cleared his throat. Tim nodded so fast his head hurt. Dean sighed. "Okay. I'll be back at five-thirty."

He shoved out the door.

She glanced at Tim. "What's his name?"

"Dean Luchetti."

"Really? I didn't think there were any Luchetti brothers left in town."

"Just Dad."

The lady stared out the window and licked her lips. "Lucky me."

"Grounded," Dean snapped as soon as Tim hopped into the car.

"I didn't do anything."

"I do not need help getting dates."

Dean was mortified. Now he had to take that gum-popping, nose-ring-wearing child to dinner. Maybe if he drove to Springfield, he'd avoid running into anyone who knew him.

"Yes, you do."

"I do what?"

"Need help. You ain't had a date since I got here, Dad."

"*Haven't* had," Dean corrected.

"That isn't healthy."

Dean blinked. "Who told you that?"

"Uncle Evan."

"He would."

"He said you could have some of his girl-friends, but none of 'em wanted to date you. How come?"

"You asked them?"

"Uncle Evan did."

Dean's fingers ached, and he realized he'd been gripping the steering wheel so tightly his knuckles had gone white. He forced himself to relax and to breathe. "When was this?"

"When he was home."

Evan had come back to Gainsville the previous year. Depressed because the love of his life wouldn't love him back, he'd been overjoyed when Jilly had shown up and proposed. Dean hadn't seen Evan since the last Luchetti family wedding, which was going to be the very last one at the rate Dean was dating.

"No wonder all the women in this town have been refusing to look me in the eye. They think I'm desperate."

"You are."

Dean ground his teeth as he started the truck. "You will not ask women out for me anymore. Is that clear?"

"Yep. But you'll never get married this way. Even I know you gotta date before you can get married."

CHAPTER NINE

DEAN'S MOTHER WAS SO THRILLED Dean had a date he barely made it out of the house. She couldn't quit giving him advice.

"Don't be rude. Don't be sarcastic. Don't burp. Don't scratch."

"What about picking my teeth with the steak knife?"

"Don't do that, either."

"Mom, I'm not a complete social reject."

"Could have fooled me."

"Thanks. Great. That helps."

She followed him onto the porch and cupped his face in her calloused hands. Until a few years ago, his mom hadn't been much for huggy-kissy. She'd had all she could manage just keeping six kids fed, clothed and out of trouble. Lately, she over-did herself trying to make amends.

"You're a catch." She kissed him on the mouth. "Always were."

"Thanks, Mommy."

Ellie swatted Dean on the behind as he walked away, a lot more lightly than she used to.

Dean picked up his date, who turned out to be older than Dean had thought—twenty-four instead of seventeen—in his truck. He didn't have anything else.

Tammy wasn't impressed. Not with that or with his jeans, clean blue shirt and good shoes.

She'd managed to change into tight black pants and a red blouse, which ended well above her belly button—also pierced.

"Where would you like to go?" he asked.

"Paris, but since that ain't happening—" She lit a cigarette without asking if he minded.

Dean hit the automatic button on the windows. "How about Perth's?"

"Sure."

The restaurant was a good one—rustic setting on the creek outside of town. Since it was Sunday, they didn't have any trouble getting a table, although the odd looks they received while walking to it made Dean squirm.

"You come here much?" Tammy asked.

"No."

"They seem to know you."

"Everyone knows everyone here."

"Doesn't that stink?"

Dean blinked. "I think it's nice."

Tammy rolled her eyes and Dean wondered how fast he could eat and get rid of her.

Pretty fast, it turned out. Since he couldn't be rude or sarcastic, his conversational skills were pretty slim. Dean knew about animals and farming. Tammy, even though she worked in a pet store and lived in Gainsville, couldn't have cared less about either one.

"Why are you here?" Dean asked.

"This was as far as the bus would take me on the cash I had."

"You don't plan to stay?"

She made a face. "Are you nuts?"

Why did every woman Dean met want to get out of town, and subsequently away from him, as fast as she could? Must be his charming personality.

"I like it here," he said. "I'd never live anywhere else."

"Good for you." Tammy slammed back the rest of her drink. "Ready?"

Since saying "definitely" was probably rude, though it would be honest, Dean paid the check and drove Tammy home. She lived in an apartment directly over the pet store, which explained how she'd been able to change clothes before he picked her up.

"Thanks for dinner."

Dean opened his mouth to say "Anytime," then snapped it shut again. Why lie?

Tammy got out and walked away without a goodbye. Dean put his truck into gear and drove toward home. It wasn't until he'd passed the woman standing in front of the coffee shop with a suitcase in her hand that he recognized Stella. Dean gaped and hit the brakes.

But when he glanced in his rearview mirror, all he saw was the tail end of her coat as she hurried inside.

Dean frowned. Had she seen him and

Tammy? Most likely. And what she'd seen had looked like a whole lot more than what it was.

His gaze lifted to the lit window above the shop. Obviously Stella had done what she'd promised and moved out. He considered banging on the door, explaining things, but why? They were friends. What difference did it make if he took the pet shop girl out to dinner?

None.

Dean lifted his foot from the brake and continued home.

So why did he feel so guilty about it?

STELLA COULDN'T BELIEVE she'd stood on the street and watched Dean with another woman. Even worse, the sight had upset her more than anything had since—

Stella slammed that door in her mind. She was not going *there* again. Since returning to Gainsville she'd refused to think about what had happened to her in L.A. and she'd begun to feel better and better. Maybe not thinking about the attack was the cure, instead of constantly rehashing it. Who'd have thought?

She realized she was staring at Dean's truck, and when the brake lights flared, she fled.

Stella hurried up the stairs and into her apartment, carrying all that she'd brought to town stuffed into a single, albeit large, suitcase.

"Idiot," she muttered.

Dean probably dated a lot of women.

And who could blame him? He was a handsome, single man in a town with far too few of them.

Stella set her suitcase in the bedroom, walked into the living room and stared out the window.

She wasn't going to be able to watch Dean dating other women, kissing other women, sleeping with other women—and not be hurt. But how was she going to avoid it? Start walking around with her eyes closed?

She'd asked him to be her friend; a friend was what she wanted. Which meant he was going to date other women, and she'd just have to get used to it. But Stella wasn't sure if she could.

She pulled out her cell phone and checked the time—7:00 p.m. in L.A. So she dialed her boss.

"Stella," he boomed. "How are you?"

Ken Abacore was a big, bluff, hearty man who, she'd been surprised to discover, had spent his twenties and thirties teaching first grade. He'd been very good at it. Then, like Stella, he'd decided he wanted something different and had worked his way up the administrative ranks.

"I'm terrific, Ken," she said. "In fact, I'm wondering if I could come back to work soon."

Over the nearly two thousand miles separating them, Stella heard Ken's good cheer deflate.

"Have you been cleared by your doctor?"

Stella hadn't seen her doctor, since the woman practiced in L.A., and she certainly wasn't going to see another one here. She cringed at the thought of explaining, again, what had happened to her.

"Not yet," she answered.

"Get back to me when you are."

"But—"

"No buts, Stella. You weren't able to do your job. We both know it. In truth, I'm not sure I'll be able to put you back in the same school."

"What?"

Stella winced at the loud, shrieky quality of her voice. *That* would certainly convince Ken she was mentally ready to return to work.

"The kids know you were attacked. They know you couldn't cope. I'm not sure they'll respect your authority anymore."

"I'll just have to make them."

"Can you?"

Stella went silent. She wasn't sure. Any type of confrontation since "the incident" had paralyzed her. Except confrontation with her dad, her mom, Dean, the kids in the school here, which didn't bother her. How odd.

"Maybe," she said.

"'Maybe' isn't good enough. Law of the jungle, kiddo. Only the strong survive. Those kids will eat you alive on a maybe."

Ken was right.

"Okay. I guess I need a little more time."

"There you go. What are you doing during your vacation?"

Stella was tempted to point out that an enforced vacation really wasn't a vacation, but she refrained.

"I've taken a temporary job as the principal of an elementary school in my hometown."

"Really?" His voice became guarded. "How's that going?"

"Not bad."

"Do you like it?"

Stella considered the question, then answered honestly. "I don't hate it."

"I'm sure you're wonderful at the job, Stella. A smaller town, smaller problems. A calmer, saner, more peaceful world. Maybe you should stay."

"Are you telling me my job is gone?"

"Of course not. I'm just telling you to think about doing something else. I've seen it happen before. When people are physically attacked, it's very difficult to get their chutzpah back."

"Chutzpah?"

"Yiddish. Great word. It means—"

"I know what it means, and I'll get it back. You'll see."

"I hope so."

After the appropriate goodbyes, Stella disconnected the call, then she sat in her rented apartment and thought about her temporary job, the rift with her father, the odd relationship with Dean. Why had she come back here again?

Oh, yeah, for the peace and quiet.

Her doorbell chose that minute to ring and Stella rubbed her eyes.

So far that was working out real well.

STELLA CONSIDERED IGNORING the doorbell, half afraid she'd find Dean on her stoop, and she didn't want to talk to him.

But the bell rang again, and she heard a woman's voice shouting her name. Stella opened the door and Linda and Laura spilled into the room.

"We come bringing food," Linda said.

"Housewarming!" Laura announced, and shut the door behind her.

"But I'm not—"

Stella stopped just short of saying she wasn't staying. They knew that. They were being friendly, and the gesture was so unexpected, so welcome, her eyes got misty.

"Hey, what's the matter?" Linda asked. "Is this a bad time?"

"No." Stella swiped at her eyes. "I was just—"

"What?" Laura asked.

She glanced back and forth between the two women. "Lonely."

"Not anymore."

They ate cheese and crackers, then some popcorn. Though Laura had been married since high school and had older children, Linda was divorced, with a younger one, and Stella had never been married and had no child at all, as sometimes happens with women, they fit.

By the time Linda and Laura left, the three women had the basis of a solid friendship. Stella didn't feel lonely anymore. She could easily imagine herself calling them on the phone, or communicating with them via e-mail once she returned to L.A. If she ever did.

It had been so long since she'd made new friends, since she'd made good friends, Stella drifted around her apartment, tidying up, and did a little twirly dance.

She was starting to like it here.

TIM STAYED AWAKE UNTIL his dad came to pick him up at the big house. He wanted to know if he had a new mommy or if he needed to keep lookin'.

"How was the date, son?" Grampa John asked.

"Women," Dean muttered. "They make no sense."

Uh-oh. That didn't sound good.

Tim got out of bed and crept to the open window so he could hear Grampa and Dad better as they sat on the porch.

"I don't think women are required to make sense," Grampa said.

"They should be."

"And who's gonna make 'em?"

His dad sighed. "Good point."

"So what went wrong?"

"What didn't?"

"Mmm," Grampa murmured. "No second date?"

"No way. She can't wait to get out of Gainsville."

Tim frowned. Why would anyone want to leave?

"That's a problem you're gonna have. Lifers are already married. Transplants don't stay."

"Why?"

"Got me," Grampa said. "What's not to love?"

"I need to talk to Tim."

Tim ducked below the windowsill.

"I gave the kid the pig. Talk about it to me."

"Huh? Oh! Not about that. If Mom didn't have a stroke about it, I guess I can't."

"I wonder how Tim got it into his head that he wanted a pet pig."

"Probably my fault. I said pigs were my favorite animals. I meant for lunch."

Tim winced. He knew pigs became pork and cows beef and sheeps mutton, but he didn't like to think about it. If he did, he'd never eat again. Besides, if he was going to be a farmer, when he was done quarterbacking in the NFL, he had to get over his attachment to a food group.

"If you don't want to talk about Wilbur, then what do you want to talk to him about?" Grampa asked.

Tim leaned forward. If he knew ahead of time what he was in trouble for, he might be able to work out an excuse.

"I can't have the kid walking up to every woman in Gainsville and asking them if they want to be his mommy."

Grampa chuckled. "That's how he got you to be his daddy."

"Which was fine. But I don't want to go on a dating spree. I'm just not good at it."

"The kid needs a mother, Dean."

"Why? He's got me, and Mom and you, and Kim and Brian and Zsa-Zsa. What's the problem?"

"Maybe you should ask him?"

"I thought I was doing a good job."

"You are."

"I thought I'd be enough for him."

"He's a little boy. Nothing's ever enough."

"You think that's it? You think maybe he'll get over this mommy obsession?"

"I think it's a mommy quest. Just like you were the daddy quest."

"Argh," Dad muttered.

"Yeah," Grampa said, and he seemed to be laughing, or trying not to.

"When that kid makes up his mind—"

"You're toast."

"I don't want to marry some woman just to give him a mom."

"And you shouldn't," Grampa said.

"Tell Tim that."

"He knows. He wants you to be happy."

"Good luck," Dad muttered.

"Why don't you say what's really bothering you, son? Stella's back in town."

Tim frowned. *Stella?* Wasn't that Ms. O'Connell's first name?

"Why would Stella being back in town bother me?"

Yeah, why? Tim thought.

"You think we didn't know about the two of you?"

"Know what?" Dad asked, but his voice sounded weird.

"She was over here a lot that last semester. I know she tutored you in math, but she kept coming even in the summer."

"So?"

"I'm not as slow as I act," Grampa said. "You two had something going on. And if I don't miss my guess, you wouldn't mind it to be going on again."

"She's Tim's principal."

"She's an old flame, and a very nice-looking single woman."

"Who isn't going to stay."

"You sure about that?"

"As sure as I was the last time she left."

"But she came back. That has to mean something."

"She didn't come back for me."

"Positive?"

"Yes."

Tim tried to make sense of what he was hearing. His dad and Ms. O'Connell had something going on? Tim had an idea of what that meant, and it kind of made him sick in the stomach. Kissing was so gross!

But he could get over that if Ms. O'Connell made his dad happy. Tim had to find a lady who was a great mom *and* a good wife. Could Ms. O'Connell be her?

Tim bit his lip and considered how he could figure such a thing out. It didn't take him long to come up with an idea. Not only could he get his dad and Ms. O'Connell to spend more time together, but he could spend time with her and see if she was mommy material.

All he had to do was stop tryin' so hard to behave. Within a few days he'd have his own chair.

Right in the principal's office.

CHAPTER TEN

ALL HELL BROKE LOOSE the following week. Stella shouldn't have been surprised, but she was. She'd thought nothing ever happened at Gainsville Elementary. She couldn't have been more wrong.

Strangely, right in the middle of every scuffle, there was Tim Luchetti. What had gotten into the boy?

On Monday morning there was an argument in gym class about the Bears and the Packers. Someone called Aaron Rodgers a name that shall not be repeated, and Tim kicked the offending cretin in the shin.

Monday lunch was the scene of a food fight, with Tim bearing the brunt and needing to be reclothed in donated items from head to toe.

Tuesday morning Tim couldn't sit still in math class and was sent to the office for walking around and around, disturbing others.

Wednesday he got distracted after going to the bathroom, and his teacher found him, an hour later, playing basketball alone on the playground.

By Thursday, when he "accidentally" tangled the hair of the girl who sat at the desk in front of him into the spokes of her chair so badly the ends had to be cut free, Tim was spending at least an hour a day in Stella's office. Laura began to refer to the cherry-wood ladder-back in the corner as Tim's Chair.

"I think he might have a crush on you," she said, before letting him in again.

Too bad Stella couldn't say "like father, like son."

Tim didn't appear contrite, but then he never did. In truth, his crimes were minor. There were just so many of them.

"Tim..." she began.

"I know. Keep my hands to myself. But she always flips her hair on my desk. Hits me in the face, slides all over my paper. It's annoying."

"I bet," Stella agreed.

Tim looked surprised.

"But that doesn't mean you can wrap Jenny's hair around the chair eight hundred times."

"'Kay."

Stella stifled a smile. If only all her problem children could be half as cute and just as agreeable.

"You gonna call my dad?" he asked.

Each time he'd come in here this week he'd asked the same question. And every time she'd said the same thing.

"Not yet."

Tim shrugged and sat on his chair.

Stella probably should have called Dean when they reached basketball-on-the-playground day, but she hadn't been able to. She didn't want to see him. She wasn't sure she could look into his eyes and not remember the sight of him with another woman.

Stupid, but true. However, if Tim continued to act up, she'd have to swallow her unease and call Dean.

"You need to behave, Tim."

"I know."

"What's gotten into you?"

"Not sure."

"Mmm," she said, and went back to work.

Her intercom buzzed. "Stella?"

Laura had given up calling her Ms. O'Connell after two days, for which Stella was grateful. Since they'd shared crackers and girl talk, Stella would have felt foolish being addressed that way by a friend.

"Ms. Hornbe is sending down two boys. One called the other gay, then that one punched the other's lights out to prove he wasn't."

"All right." Stella sighed. "What is it with all this gay stuff?"

She'd had several kids sent in for using the word derogatorily and several more for taking offense to it.

"I think kids are afraid," Tim said.

Stella blinked. "Of what?"

"That they're gay."

"A five-year-old is afraid of being gay?" She had a hard time believing that, but—

"I don't think they know what gay is yet," Tim said, "but they hear the word and

they can tell it isn't a good thing—or that
people don't think it's a good thing—but
no one will tell 'em what it is, you know?
So they get afraid."

Amazingly, that made sense.

"What should I do about it?" she murmured.

Stella wasn't really asking Tim but
thinking out loud. He answered, anyway.

"You should tell 'em what the word
means. Then they won't be scared anymore."

"I don't think I can do that."

"How come?"

"That's for their parents to tell them."

"Then make 'em do it."

Stella doubted she could make anyone do
anything. However, Tim had a point. If the
little kids who were throwing around the
word so freely knew what it meant, knew
the word had little to do with them, at least
right now, maybe they wouldn't use it so
much. At any rate, asking their parents to
explain things was not a bad idea.

"You can return to class, Tim," she said.

"Okay."

He jumped off the chair.

"I don't want to see you in here again today."

"I'll try."

Stella narrowed her eyes, but either Tim didn't feel her glare on his retreating back, or he didn't care. She didn't think he tried, either, since he appeared at her door early the next morning.

"What did I tell you?" she demanded.

"That you didn't want to see me in here yesterday. And you didn't." He sat in his chair.

"Are you *trying* to get in trouble, Tim?"

"Me?"

He presented her with his wide-eyed Howdy Doody face and folded his hands in his lap. He hadn't answered her question, but she let it pass.

"What did you do this time?"

"Spit in the fish tank."

"Why?"

"They like it! Fish come after spit. Then you can see 'em better. But Mrs. Neville isn't from here. She doesn't know stuff. She didn't believe me."

"I'm from here, and I didn't know that."

Tim shrugged. "Maybe it's a guy thing."

"I'd say."

He jumped off his chair and crossed to her desk, glancing at the notes on her blotter. "What have you been doing since yesterday?"

She lifted her brows. "You want me to tell you who got in trouble?"

"Nah. I know that already. I wondered what you were gonna do about stuff."

"Why?"

"To tell you the truth, Ms. O'Connell—" he heaved an exaggerated sigh "—you're not doin' so good."

She stiffened. "What?"

"You never did this before, did you?"

"I was a principal. I *am* a principal."

"Of little kids?"

"Well, no."

"I didn't think so." He shook his head. "You don't get it."

"Get what?"

"How to handle stuff."

"What's there to get? A kid screws up, I punish him or her."

"There's more to stuff than messin' up. Like Jess."

"Who?"

"Jessica Flanders."

"The girl who won't do her homework?"

"Not won't. *Can't.* Her mom and dad made Mrs. Little skip her a grade."

Stella rarely agreed to children skipping a level. Even if they were intelligent enough, their social skills were usually sadly lacking, which only made for deeper problems. Nowadays most schools had a gifted and talented program so all children would feel challenged while remaining in their age group.

"That's inappropriate," Stella said.

"Okay." Tim answered in a voice that clearly revealed he had no idea what she was talking about. "Jess should be in my grade. She doesn't get anything that's goin' on in her class. She cries in the bathroom at lunchtime."

"Oh, no," Stella murmured.

"Yeah. So she shouldn't be punished." His expression became considering. "Maybe you could ground her parents."

"Wouldn't that be nice? But I doubt it. I will talk to them." Stella made a note. She glanced at Tim, bit her lip, then gave a mental shrug. She could use the help. "Anything else?"

"Mickey Malfre."

"Little kid, big mouth. Likes to run with scissors."

"That's him."

"He can't stay quiet in class."

"I think he needs a pill."

Stella frowned. "What kind of pill?"

"The kind I get, except with Mickey, he might need two."

"You think he's got ADHD?"

"He's got somethin'," Tim muttered.

"No one's tested him?"

"I dunno. But he doesn't take a chill pill. All of us kids who take them come to see Mrs. Benedict at lunch."

A school nurse had handled the dispensing of medications back when the budget had included one. Now the county health nurse stopped by a few days a month. Which meant Laura got to give out the chill pills at lunchtime.

Stella made a note to speak with Mickey's teacher, who could in turn speak with his parents. ADHD often slipped through the cracks because it was hard to diagnose in younger children. The earmarks of the disease—lack of attention and inability to focus—were all too common in those under five.

"Any other disasters in the making?" she asked.

"Nope. Just remember that little kids don't know they're screwin' up. They don't mean to. Not yet, anyway."

Stella *had* been treating the little kids like the big ones—as if they knew and completely understood the rules and were therefore breaking them on purpose just to see if they could. They probably weren't.

She contemplated Tim. Except, maybe, for this one.

He stared at her from between his overly long bangs. "You gonna call my dad?"

"I don't think that's necessary. Just don't spit in the fish tank anymore."

Tim sighed and shuffled away, feet dragging, head hanging, then he slammed the door behind him.

A week ago, Stella would have gone after any kid who'd done that and read him the riot act. But if she'd learned one thing, it was that the force of closing a door was in direct proportion to the age of a child. The younger they were, the harder they slammed.

So why did it seem as if that particular slam had been aimed at her?

Maybe she did need to talk to Dean.

DEAN WHEELED INTO THE school parking lot, caught sight of a bunch of people on the soccer field at the far end and cut straight across to park near the grass.

Tonight was Tim's first football game.

His parents were right behind him. Kim, Brian and Zsa-Zsa were coming, too. He only hoped all those people wouldn't make Tim so nervous he didn't pay attention to the game.

Dean jumped out of his car, trotted across the empty space and took a position on the sidelines with the other parents. He never knew what to say to them.

He'd come into the parenting universe late, dragging along a child he'd never diapered. They'd gone through everything from the beginning, and just like most other areas of his life, Dean didn't fit in.

The day was perfect for a peewee football game. Bright and sunny, with just enough chill so the kids wouldn't get overheated in their gear.

The other team looked huge. Or maybe that was just because Tim looked so small. Even wearing shoulder pads, knee pads, thigh pads, hip pads and forearm pads, Tim probably weighed sixty pounds. Dean already regretted allowing Tim to play, and they hadn't even kicked off yet.

"Hey." Stella's voice at his elbow made Dean jump. "Whoops! Sorry I startled you."

"It's okay. I was lost in thought."

Dean gave Stella a quick once-over. She looked happy, healthy, in control. Whatever had happened to her, she was doing a great job repressing it. He wasn't a psychiatrist, but that couldn't be good.

Dean sighed. He wasn't her husband, or even her boyfriend; he definitely wasn't her doctor. He was her friend.

Dean gritted his teeth. He hated being friendly.

"About what?" Stella asked.

For an instant, Dean blanked. *About what, what?* Then he remembered. He'd been lost in thought about—

"What possessed me to say yes to peewee football?"

"What did?"

"Temporary insanity. And the kid really, really loves the game."

"Kids really, really love a lot of things. That doesn't mean they get to do them."

He stuck his tongue out at her, and she laughed. "Sorry. Giving advice is an occupational hazard. If it helps, I've been told by countless football coaches, as well as nurses and doctors, that there are more sports injuries in basketball than football."

"Really?"

She lifted her hand. "Honest."

"Thanks." Dean let out a breath. "That does help."

They went silent as the thud of a cleat against pigskin sent the football toppling end over end across the grass, instead of through the air, before smacking some hapless eight-year-old in the shin like an out of control spin the bottle. At least the boy was smart enough to fall on the ball rather than try and run with it. The other team was far too close for that.

"Tim ask you to his game?" Dean asked.

"No. I saw you."

Dean's mood lightened. Until he remembered the last time she'd seen him, and he wanted to run, like some kid was now doing on the field, as if wolves were nipping at his heels.

Thunk.

Someone hit the child from behind and he flew. So did the ball.

"Ouch," Stella murmured.

"Yeah." Dean slid a glance her way. She didn't seem mad. "I should explain—"

At the same time she blurted, "There's a problem—"

They both went silent.

"You first," Stella said.

"No, you. A problem with Tim?"

"I'm not sure."

Tim trotted onto the field. He was playing defense? Oh, brother! This should be good. Or very, very bad.

He glanced at Stella. "What did he do?"

"Which day?"

Dean's eyes widened. "He's done something every day?"

"Sometimes twice a day."

"And you're just telling me now!"

Dean's voice was too loud. Several other parents turned to stare. He waved at them and they stopped.

"He didn't do anything major, and it wasn't until today that I figured out he was getting into trouble on purpose. I'm just not sure why."

The play was called. The kids scrambled. Tim knocked one huge beast on his behind and headed for the quarterback.

Dean stopped listening to Stella and stepped closer, craning his head to see what would happen.

Tim flattened that kid, too.

Several of the other dads turned around and gave Dean a thumbs-up. He returned the gesture.

"What was that?" Stella asked.

"Tim sacked the quarterback."

"That's good?"

"If you're a defensive end, it is."

"Okay. Can we get back to why Tim is being a pain?"

Dean sighed. "I have an idea. Did he ask you to be his mom?"

"What?" she said, a little too loudly herself. "No!"

"He didn't ask you to date me?"

Stella frowned. "No."

"Hmm. That's weird."

Dean returned his attention to the field. Tim was watching them. He waved and his son waved back, then got into position for the next play.

"Why is that weird?" Stella asked.

"He's on a mommy quest."

"A what?"

Dean turned slightly, became fascinated with the slight blush in her cheeks and the way the wind stirred her short hair. When the sun hit it just right, Stella's hair shone more red than brown. Why hadn't he noticed that before?

How was he ever going to be friends with this woman?

"I'm sorry," he said. "What did you ask me?"

"What's a mommy quest?"

"Just what it sounds like. Search for a mommy."

"And he does this how?"

"By asking every single woman he meets if she wants the job. Or at least that's how he went about his daddy quest."

She blinked. "Let me get this straight— he asked you to be his dad and you said yes?"

"Not at first. At first, he kind of freaked me out."

"I bet."

Dean grinned. "But then he grows on you."

"And now he's decided he needs a mom."

"Yeah."

"So he's asking women to be his

mommy." Understanding lit her face. "Like he did with that delivery woman at the party."

"Right."

Tim had also blabbed a description of Dean's ideal woman.

He let his gaze wander over Stella again. Which was so far from the truth it wasn't even funny.

"Since then he seems to have decided he'd do better to find me a wife. He's been setting me up."

Stella lifted an eyebrow. "Really?"

"Which is what you saw this weekend."

She looked away. "That was none of my business."

"Tim asked the pet-shop girl out, and I couldn't very well say no."

Stella stared down her nose at him, which was pretty hard considering he was taller than her, but she managed. "I just bet you couldn't."

"I'm sorry you had to move out of your parents' house."

"I wanted to. My father and I do not get along."

"Been there, done that."

She'd just begun to smile, a slight tilt of her lips, a lightening in her eyes, when a shout went up from the crowd and her gaze shot behind him. She began to run.

Dean turned. Then he ran, too.

THE FIRST RULE OF FOOTBALL was *pay attention*. Tim knew that. But payin' attention was hard. Especially when his dad and Ms. O'Connell seemed to be getting along so great. He couldn't stop sneakin' glances at them, and then someone snuck up on him and—

Wham!

Tim flew forward and smacked into the ground. That wouldn't have been so bad; except there was another kid there first and his shoe crunched Tim right beneath the ribs.

He tried to get up, but he couldn't breathe. Tried to tell the other guys, the coach, all the faces that stared at him, that he was fine, except he couldn't talk. Then Ms. O'Connell was there, and she knew what to do.

"Tim, did you get the wind knocked out of you?"

He'd gotten something knocked out of him, but he didn't think it was the wind. Maybe his stuffing. He'd heard about having the stuffing knocked out of you, and he'd figured that had to hurt.

He hurt. In fact, he thought this might be what dyin' felt like, and if it was, no wonder no one ever wanted to.

"Move your feet," she ordered.

He did.

"Hands."

Those, too.

"Neck hurt?"

He shook his head.

Relief passed over her face. What was she so relieved about? He still couldn't breathe, and his lungs felt like they might go *kaboom*.

"Tim!"

His dad was there, and the kids and the coach moved back. When he stared up all he could see was Dean and Ms. O'Connell and, behind them, the bluest blue sky ever.

"He can move everything," Ms. O'Connell

said. "I think he got the wind knocked out of him."

"There's only one remedy for that," his dad said.

Reaching down, he grabbed Tim by the belt and hoisted his middle off the ground, then lowered him, then lifted him again.

"Hey!" Ms. O'Connell smacked his dad's arm.

But suddenly Tim could breathe again, and he did with a huge gasp.

"I—I'm okay," he said, and sat up.

The crowd and his teammates cheered. He kind of liked that.

He also liked it when Ms. O'Connell removed his helmet and wiped his face with a tissue from her pocket and some water from a bottle. Then she kissed his damp forehead. Right there in front of everyone.

"You okay now?" she asked.

Tim was more than okay. He was in love.

CHAPTER ELEVEN

TIM WENT BACK INTO THE GAME, even though his dad said he didn't have to, and Ms. O'Connell had a hissy.

"Take him home, Dean," she ordered.

Tim shook his head. "What kind of wussy doesn't play after he's gotten the wind knocked out of him?"

"I don't know—" his dad socked him in the arm lightly "—what kind?"

"Not a Luchetti kind." He gave his dad a high five.

As Tim was running onto the field, he heard Ms. O'Connell say, "All men are nuts."

His dad just laughed.

Tim saw his gramma and grampa, his aunt and uncle and his cousin arrive, but he'd learned his lesson and paid better attention to the game after that. If he got knocked down too hard again his dad would make him stop playing, and Tim liked football, he really, really liked it.

He might be little, but he was fast and he was tough. For the first time in his life, Tim was good at something. He was part of a team, and while he couldn't say that any of the guys were his friends yet, he kind of thought they might be soon.

Tim's team won and he ran toward his family, disappointed to discover Ms. O'Connell had left. "Where'd she go?"

His dad's gaze narrowed. "Who?"

"Ms. O'Connell."

"She had to work, and we have to talk."

"Why?" he asked, but he knew.

"Let's have hamburgers and ice cream at Schully's to celebrate," Grampa said.

"Count us out." Aunt Kim jerked her thumb at a sleeping Zsa-Zsa.

"Did she see any of my game at all?" Tim asked, touching his cousin's tiny hand with his much bigger one.

"Didn't you hear her screaming your name?"

"No."

"You must be the only one, then," Uncle Brian muttered.

"I'm going to buy her a cheerleading outfit," Aunt Kim decided. "With pom-poms."

"Oh, no." Uncle Brian shook his head. "Here we go."

"She'll love it!"

"She'd love to play with matches, too, but that doesn't mean we buy her a box."

Aunt Kim turned away from Uncle Brian so she could lean down and brush a fingertip over Tim's nose. "Silver and blue, just like your uniform. She'll be cute, don't you think?"

"Sure," he said, though he wasn't exactly *sure.* Zsa-Zsa could be cute, but she could also be a really, really, really big pain.

Tim saw Uncle Brian watching him, and when he winked, Tim knew he thought the exact same thing.

"Hamburgers and ice cream for dinner," his dad announced. "My treat."

"Yay!" Tim leaped into the air, then started after his gramma.

Dean grabbed him by the back of the jersey. "You come with me."

"Rats."

"Uh-huh."

Tim took off his shoulder pads and stuck his face mask through the head hole so he could carry it like everyone else did. He climbed into the truck, then he waited for the lecture. His dad hadn't even driven out of the parking lot before he started.

"I heard you've been in the office every day this week."

"Yep."

"Why?"

Tim put on an innocent face. "Maybe I need my meds adjusted."

Dean's eyes narrowed. "I don't think so."

Tim glanced out the window, wondering if he could stall until they got to Schully's. He doubted it.

"I know what you're up to, Tim. Ms. O'Connell is your principal. We aren't going to date."

"Why not? Principals date, too." He frowned. "Don't they?"

"I suspect so. But Ms. O' Connell and I. We— Uh— She and I were—"

"What?"

"We dated before, and it didn't work out."

"So?"

"We're friends. That's the best way."

"What if you were friendly daters? Isn't that better?"

"No."

"But she's all alone." He thought of the soft way her hands had checked him over to make sure he wasn't broken, how she'd touched his face, kissed his forehead. "I think she needs a family."

And if she didn't, Tim did. Or at least a slightly larger family than what he already had. One mommy more ought to do it.

His dad swallowed as if his throat hurt. "No, Tim. She doesn't need a family. She's not the type of woman who stays in a place like this. She doesn't marry a farmer. Or adopt his son."

"Why not?"

"She just doesn't."

From the stubborn set of his mouth, Dad wasn't going to listen to any arguments. His mind was made up.

But so was Tim's.

He'd never felt the way he had when he'd been lying on the ground and seen their two faces above him. In that moment, something had gone *click,* and Tim had understood that Ms. O'Connell was his heart-mom, the one who would take care of them forever. The only problem was, how would he convince her, and his dad, of that?

He stared out the window as Dean drove the short distance from the school to the ice-cream shop on the other side of town, and he remembered something his teacher had told the class that week.

She'd been talking about writing stories, but he figured the same rules applied to real life, since stories were supposed to tell about life, only prettied up.

Show, don't tell, she'd said. It was a good rule.

Tim couldn't *tell* his dad how perfect Ms. O'Connell was for them, he'd have to *show* him.

And Tim knew exactly how.

DEAN WATCHED TIM DOWN two cheeseburgers, a chocolate milkshake and large fries. "Your gut okay?"

Tim lifted his T-shirt. Despite the huge meal, his skinny belly lay flat beneath the waistband of his football pants. The imprint of a football cleat, dark red and deepening toward purple, marred the skin over his bony ribs.

"What is that?" Dean roared.

"Watch it!" Gramma ordered.

"Look at his stomach, Mom."

Ellie leaned over and ran the tip of her finger over the mark. Tim giggled and Dean relaxed. He couldn't be broken inside if he was laughing. Still—

"Maybe I should get him X-rayed. He could have cracked a rib."

His dad snorted; his mom shook her head. "If he went back in the game, his rib isn't broken."

"Is that so, doctor?" Dean asked.

"I've seen enough broken to know."

That was certainly true.

"You should put some ice on it, though." She stood. "Thanks for dinner."

The requisite hugs and kisses ensued. Then Dean and Tim threw away their trash and headed for the door.

"Gotta pee," Tim said. "I'll meet you in the car."

Since that happened a lot, Dean went outside as Tim dashed into the bathroom.

Dean thought about the game, his talk with Stella, the fear when Tim had gone down and he hadn't gotten back up. Having Stella there had helped. He wished she would stay here forever, but he had to stop wishing that.

Despite whatever trouble she'd had in L.A., she planned to go back. She said her job was her life—and she hadn't meant this one.

Maybe he should start power dating. At least he'd get her out of his mind for a few hours a night.

Dean glanced up just as Tim waved goodbye to June Renfrew, the owner of the ice-cream store. A widow, she'd been running the place on her own since her husband passed away about a year ago. Her daughter had been a few years ahead of Dean in school. He thought Bobby might have dated her, but he couldn't remember. June lifted her hand, and Dean did the same.

Strange. He didn't think she even knew him. Of course, this was Gainsville, where everyone knew everyone, as well as their dogs.

A few minutes later Dean wheeled into his driveway, wincing when Bear, four doodles, Cubby and a partridge in a pear tree—began to bark and chase the truck.

"We need to get rid of a few dogs," he muttered.

"No." Tim's eyes were wide. "Who would you pick?"

"Eenie, Meenie, Meinie or Mo."

Which was what they'd named the four remaining puppies, who weren't exactly puppies anymore, even though they acted like it.

"Not them!" Tim's lip trembled.

"Relax, kid, I won't. I just dream big. Now, get an ice pack and do your homework."

"But it's Friday!"

"If you do it now, then you can goof off the entire weekend."

Tim frowned as he thought about it, then a smile spread over his entire face. "You're so smart, Dad."

Dean was warmed by the sentiment, and he never got tired of hearing it. Maybe because the older his son got, the dumber Dean would become, at least in Tim's eyes.

Tim loped off to the kitchen, Cubby on his heels. The freezer door opened, then closed. Since Tim had arrived, Dean kept half a dozen professional ice packs frozen at all times.

An hour later, Dean was watching TV when Tim ran through the house, feet pounding as loudly as a herd of elephants. "I gotta feed Wilbur."

"Now?"

"Gramma said I should feed him whenever I'm home, which ain't been much lately." Tim bounced on the tips of his toes. "I don't want to make her angry."

He banged out of the house and ran through the cornfield. Kid must really be worried about upsetting his gramma, and Dean couldn't say that he blamed him.

Not more than a minute later, a vehicle

turned into Dean's lane. He figured Brian, but he didn't recognize the car. He did recognize the woman behind the wheel.

June Renfrew from the ice-cream store. He didn't think she was coming here to ask his favorite flavor, either. Or maybe she was.

Dean winced. The woman had to be twenty-five years his senior.

His gaze turned toward his parents' farm. Tim was lucky he wasn't within grabbing distance.

STELLA STAYED LATE AT school. After she watched part of the football game, she stopped by choir, then intramural volleyball, strolled through the halls and spoke with a few teachers, who'd also stayed late, then made some phone calls to parents who worked and could not be reached during the day.

When she finished she walked to her apartment—a twice-daily trip she'd come to enjoy. On the way to school she went over her schedule, on her way home she thought about her day. She'd be disappointed when it became too cold to walk.

Stella frowned as she turned onto Main Street. Where had that thought come from? She wasn't going to be here when the snow flew. No way.

She ran up the steps to her apartment—pleasantly tired from a job well done, rather than exhausted by a job that never ended—and unlocked the door. No matter how safe Gainsville was, she could not get out of the habit of locking everything.

Over the past week Stella had begun to feel both calmer and stronger, at home in a place that had never been home before. When she walked to and from school, people greeted her on the street. Parents stopped her to discuss their children, and she knew which ones they meant. She didn't have to go to her computer and look them up.

The friendship she'd forged with Laura and Linda continued. They'd had dinner one night and they'd laughed and talked just as they had when they'd been at her house.

She was putting down roots here; she was starting to fit in. While that thought should panic her enough to make her run all the way back to L.A., instead she felt… happy. Until she turned to shut the door and saw the shadow of a man lurking on the landing.

Her gasp was sharp and cut through the silence like a blade through silk.

"Stella?"

Her father's voice. So why didn't she feel any less trapped?

"What are you doing here?"

"Is that any way to greet your dad?"

"Dad? Since when do you refer to yourself as Dad?"

He sighed. "I come in peace."

"I doubt that," she muttered, but she let him in.

Stella had planned to call Dean as soon as she got home and check on Tim. The boy had bounced right back into the game, but she was still concerned. As any principal would be, she told herself, even though she knew it was a lie. She was fonder of Tim than any principal should be.

Her father's gaze drifted over the rented room, the rented furniture, the bare book-case and the empty magazine rack. She hadn't had time to personalize the place yet.

He didn't make a comment. Maybe he *had* come in peace.

"I know why you left L.A."

Or not.

Stella turned away from the kitchen table, which she used as a desk since she usually ate in front of the TV, and contemplated her father. "How?"

"I called your boss. He was shocked you hadn't told your family. Frankly, so am I."

"What good would telling you do?"

"Knowing the truth made me understand why you came back here with your tail between your legs."

Stella's head came up. "I did not."

He snorted. "You accepted a job that was beneath you and took up with a man who's beneath you, too."

"I didn't take up with anyone," she said, "and I only accepted the job that you offered."

"Temporarily."

"Are you trying to say my tenure is up?"

"No." He appeared disgusted. "I've been asked to offer you the position permanently. Seems you've impressed everyone."

"Don't sound so happy about it."

"I'm not."

Stella sighed. "Father—"

"If you want to stay in Gainsville, though I have no idea why, you could come and work for me at the bank."

"Oh, yeah. That'd be fun."

"It's better than being a nose wiper."

"I haven't wiped a nose since I got here."

"That's beside the point." He took a deep breath, then let it out in a rush. "I had such plans for you, Stella."

"I know," she said. "But why?"

"Why wouldn't I? You're my only child."

"I'm happy in education. Why can't you accept that and be proud of me?"

"Because you aren't all that you can be. You were the best student Gainsville High ever had. You could have done anything."

He stared into the distance, as if seeing something far away, or perhaps long ago, and Stella understood. Why hadn't she before? Perhaps because she was too busy being angry with him.

"What did you want to be, Father?" she whispered. "Where did you want to go?"

At first he didn't answer, just continued to stare. Then he coughed, straightened and scowled. "I am what I'm supposed to be. I live where O'Connells have lived for generations."

She felt a tug of sympathy for her father, who had been trapped in a place he'd never fit, in a job he didn't like. He'd wanted her to escape. Someone had to.

But now she was back, like a bird to the cage. Stella didn't feel that way, but she could see where he might.

So, in reality, her father's annoying habit of pushing her into a job she didn't want and a life she didn't need was his way of saying he loved her.

She wished he'd just said he loved her.

"Father," she began. "Maybe you should try another line of work."

"What?" He stiffened. "I'm the president

of the bank, Stella. There isn't a better job in Gainsville."

"Maybe you could leave Gainsville."

He seemed genuinely puzzled. "How?"

"You sell your house, pack your things and go."

"I couldn't."

He fixed her with the glare that had always made her sit up straight, eat her peas, do all her homework, as well as every bit of extra credit. The only time she'd ever rebelled was with Dean. Which, now that she considered it, had given her the courage to go her own way ever since.

"*You* can leave, Stella," her father continued.

And they were right back where they started.

"I will. Eventually. Although..." Her voice drifted off as a new thought took root.

"Although what?"

"I may not go back to L.A."

"Good choice. More opportunities in New York."

"Opportunities for what?"

Being lonely in a crowd.

Seeing a psychiatrist three days a week.

Getting mugged.

"Anything," he said. "You could be anything, Stella."

She stared at him for a long moment, for the first time feeling a sense of warmth, if not *from* him, at least *for* him.

"Thanks, Dad."

CHAPTER TWELVE

FOR THE NEXT TWO WEEKS, women showed up at Dean's door with annoying regularity. He had no idea where Tim was finding them all.

Young and not so young, tall, short, thin and not so thin, blond, brunette, redhead, there was even one with locks the shade of a Smurf. They came and asked Dean out, and his mother, curse her, was usually around to say, "Go ahead. Your father and I can watch Tim," which made Dean think she was in on this somehow. Probably because she was.

Tim had even managed to finagle a date with the nurse from his pediatrician's office after Dean had taken him, against his mother's advice, to have his ribs X-rayed. Just as Eleanor had predicted, Tim was fine. Only a bruise—albeit a nasty one.

The nurse had shown up that same night in her white uniform—Dean hadn't even realized they wore those anymore—with the little hat and everything.

When Dean had pointed out that, for once, his parents weren't around, and he couldn't just leave Tim and trot off—he'd been in more restaurants over the past fourteen days than he wanted to remember—Ms. Prinkle had drawn a bottle of Jack Daniel's from her purse, which was somewhat frighteningly shaped like an old-fashioned physician's bag.

He'd had a tough time getting rid of her.

When had Dean become irresistible, anyway? The last time he'd dated—albeit quite a while ago—not too many women had been interested. All of a sudden when Tim asked, they flocked.

But really who could resist that face asking them, "Will you be my mommy?"

Not many, it appeared. Otherwise Tim had managed to zero in on the ones who thought he was adorable. When paired with a father who owned a successful farm and wasn't half bad looking, they either conveniently forgot Dean's personality problems or figured time was a-wasting and they could live with them.

In truth, now that Dean knew his attention problems and impulse-control issues were the result of adult ADHD and not stupidity, he felt better than he had in his life—or at least he had until the dating game had taken up residence on his porch.

No matter how many times he told the kid to knock it off, the women kept coming. Dean had never been more miserable.

Someone knocked on the screen door. Dean groaned.

"Wasn't me," Tim said without even glancing up.

Why hadn't the dogs barked? Must be his mother. None of them dared utter a sound in her presence. Except *she* never knocked.

"Come in!" he shouted, and the screen door opened, then shut.

The click of high heels on the hardwood floors made him frown. He sent an evil glare Tim's way, but the kid was busy examining the scab in the shape of a shoe on his rib cage. Not only did he sport a dilly of a bruise, he also had a doozy of a scrape.

A gasp from the doorway made Dean glance over so fast his neck cracked. He winced.

A strange woman with a briefcase stared in horror at Tim's injury. "You kicked him!"

"Did not," Tim answered.

Dean's lips twitched. You'd think the kid had brothers.

Angry black eyes met Dean's. "I meant you."

"I don't know who you are." Dean stood. "But—"

"Allison McCaferty, social services."

Tim let his shirt fall back over his stomach. "Uh-oh."

"You better believe it," Ms. McCaferty said.

For an instant Dean was paralyzed with uncertainty, then he forced himself to speak. "I don't remember an appointment."

"Surprise visit," Ms. McCaferty said. "We like those."

Dean glanced at Tim. The kid wasn't

afraid of much, but he was afraid of social services. His son didn't look so hot.

Dean set a hand on Tim's shoulder. "Why don't you brush your teeth and get ready for school?"

Like a zombie, Tim turned and left the room.

"Would you like to sit, Ms. McCaferty?"

She took a chair as far away from the Cheerios-and-milk explosion as she could. Dean stepped toward the sink, intending to clean up, then figured, why bother?

He sat back his seat. "Coffee?"

"No, thank you."

Dean stared at the woman. She was probably in her late twenties, though you'd never know it from her bland suit, sensible pumps and scraped-back hairstyle. She was already getting lines around her mouth from frowning, and if she didn't watch it, she'd have one between her eyes, too.

"How did Tim sustain that bruise?" Ms. McCaferty clicked the catch on her briefcase and withdrew a folder.

"Football. He fell on someone's shoe."

She nodded and made a note inside the

file. "There was a report of X-rays recently."

"For his ribs." Dean scowled. "If you knew about that, you knew what happened."

She didn't even look up. "It's best if I ask you what happened."

"So you can see if I lied?"

Now she lifted her gaze to his. "Did you?"

"Ask Tim."

"I will."

How could such a young woman have such cold eyes?

"You've been in the bars in town quite often of late. Is that a habit for you?"

"No. And they are restaurants, not bars."

"Then why were you?"

Dean considered the woman, then shrugged. "My son wants a mother. He's been setting me up with anything in a skirt."

"He isn't your son."

Dean let his own eyes cool. "He is in every way that matters."

She tried to hold his gaze, but she wasn't

quite that good yet. Dean had won show-downs with every one of his brothers. He might be hyper, but a staring contest? That just wasn't a contest.

"Why does Tim feel the need for a mother?" she asked.

"Don't all kids?"

"Perhaps. But is he in need of a champion?"

What was this woman talking about? She sounded as if she'd escaped from a nearby Renaissance Faire.

"You mean someone to protect him? From what?"

"You?"

Dean clenched his hands. "Lady, you're pressing your luck."

"Really?" She lifted her overly plucked brows. "Are you going to kick me in the ribs?"

"Dad would never hurt me."

Tim stood in the doorway.

"He isn't your dad."

"He is, and he always will be. You can take me away, and all I'll do is come back. Because I'm a Luchetti forevermore."

Tim grabbed his half-full cereal bowl from the table and upended it on Ms. McCaferty's head. Then he ran outside, letting the screen door bang behind him.

The social worker started at the sound, then calmly gathered her papers as milk and Cheerios ran down her face. "May I see the rest of the house?"

"Um, sure." Dean handed her a dish towel and went to chastise Tim.

But his son had escaped through the cornfield and there was no way Dean was going to be able to talk to him unless he wanted to shout.

Dean glanced at Ms. McCaferty, who was picking cereal out of her hair. Shouting was probably a bad idea. He'd deal with Tim later.

He ushered the woman into the living room, wincing at the mess. "Sorry. I've been a little busy."

"I heard." Ms. McCaferty stared down her nose at him.

Dean gritted his teeth to keep any sarcastic comments to himself. "Uh, yeah. Well, these are the bedrooms."

"Tim has his own?"

"Yes. It's the one—"

"With the Batman sheets." She made a check in her file, then glanced up. "And yours?"

"I prefer Scooby-Doo."

She didn't smile; she didn't even blink.

"May I take a look?" Ms. McCaferty indicated Tim's room with a nod.

"Can I stop you?"

"No."

What had happened to his vow of no sarcasm? It had lasted less than a minute. The woman bugged him.

Dean wandered into the kitchen and began cleaning up while she did whatever it was she had to do in Tim's room. A high-pitched shriek caused him to fumble, then drop a cup, which was, thankfully, empty and plastic.

He'd taken one step toward the hall when Cubby shot past and banged out the screen door. "What the…?"

Hadn't the woman ever seen a dog before?

Then Wilbur trotted through, nose in the

air, tiny hooved feet going *clippety-clop* across the wood floor.

Ms. McCaferty followed, scribbling in her folder.

"So," Dean said. "How'd I do?"

TIM WAS SCARED. When the social workers came, the news was never good.

He'd actually been behaving for a couple of weeks. Ms. O'Connell was doin' okay as principal. After a few pointers from him, she'd gotten kind of good at it. Besides, he didn't want his dad to figure out what he was up to before he got done being up to it.

But today he wanted to see her. He was nervous; he was scared. He remembered how she'd taken care of him at football, and he wanted her to take care of him again.

So Tim shot a spitball at the blackboard. The thing went splat, right next to Mrs. Neville's head. Everyone laughed.

Mrs. Neville didn't even bother to turn around, just flicked the soppy paper off the board with a fingernail and said, "Office, Tim."

Man, that was so easy.

Tim tore down the hall. As he got close to the front of the building, he heard a voice he'd heard before. "I'd like to see Principal O'Connell about Tim Luchetti."

The social worker was here! That couldn't be good.

What if she'd come to take him back? This was probably where she'd do it. Away from home, when the family wasn't looking. Away from Dean, who'd never let him go. In a place with lots of people, where Tim couldn't make a scene, though she obviously knew nothin' about kids if she believed that.

The more Tim thought about it, the more likely it seemed the social worker had come to school to collect him and make him go back to foster care. Not that he'd ever been in foster care, but he'd heard about it. He wasn't goin' there.

"Uh-uh," Tim muttered.

Mrs. Benedict glanced up and Tim ducked. If she saw him, he'd never get away.

Tim inched behind the security desk, then slid down the fifth-grade hallway, through the door and onto the playground, where he slipped into the cornfield that lined the teachers' parking lot and disappeared.

"ALLISON McCAFERTY." The social worker held out her hand.

Stella, who had dealt with her share of social workers, was surprised at the woman's youth and manner. She was stiff and formal, with more shadows in her eyes than her age warranted.

What had she seen that had put them there? And had she seen it here?

"Stella O'Connell." She gave Ms. McCaferty's slim, icy hand a brisk shake. "What can I do for you?"

"Can you tell me about Tim Luchetti?"

"Great kid. He belongs with the Luchettis."

McCaferty frowned. "I just came from a home visit. There was a pig in his room."

"That would be Wilbur."

The woman's eyes widened. "You knew?"

"Sure."

"You approve of barn animals in a child's bedroom?"

"This is a farming community. There are barn animals everywhere."

"That can't be sanitary."

"Kids are resilient, and a little dirt never hurt anyone."

"His father appeared hungover and he reeked of cigarettes."

"That doesn't sound like Dean."

"Dean?"

Stella shrugged. "We went to school together."

"You're from here?"

"Yes."

"Oh, I assumed—" She glanced at Stella's mint-green suit jacket. "I thought you'd transferred."

The words "though I can't understand why" were left unsaid.

Stella might have thought the same thing herself a few weeks ago, but now she found the attitude annoying. Her shoulders tightened. "I worked in L.A."

"Really?" Ms. McCaferty brightened minutely. "I was in Chicago until recently."

Which might have something to do with
the shadows in her eyes.

"Why did you leave?" Stella asked.

Ms. McCaferty's expression immediately dimmed. "Why did you?"

Answering a question with a question—
one of Stella's pet peeves.

"Is there a reason behind your questions?" Her voice went stiff and cool.
"Perhaps an explanation as to why my
background in L.A. has anything to do
with Tim?"

The social worker didn't appear offended
at Stella's words or tone. In her business
she no doubt heard worse every day.

"I was going to ask for your recommendation about the Luchetti case," she said.
"If you're nuts, I don't want it."

"If I was nuts, I doubt I'd be the principal of Gainsville Elementary."

"Never can tell."

Since Stella knew the woman could find
out what had happened easily enough on
her own, she told the truth.

"I was attacked by a student. Had a problem working in that venue, so I was advised

to take some time away. I came home and now I'm filling in."

"You're a substitute?"

"For the moment."

Though more and more lately she'd started to think of this job as hers.

"Your turn," Stella said.

Ms. McCaferty, who was rooting in her briefcase, glanced up. "I'm sorry?"

"I told you why I left L.A. Why did you ditch Chicago?"

The woman withdrew a folder with a tab that read Luchetti. "Everything was too much—too much work, too much sadness, too much…bad."

"You don't find that here?"

"I've only been here a month, but I'm hoping." She opened her file with an anal little snap. "Now, I saw a foot-shaped bruise on Tim's ribs."

"Football."

Ms. McCaferty lifted her gaze. "You knew about that, too, and you didn't report it?"

"I saw it happen. It was a common sports injury, nothing more."

"The child seems to have an inordinate amount of scrapes and bruises."

"He's a farm kid. They all do." Stella took a deep breath. "When I first got here I thought the same thing, but I was wrong. People like you and I, we've seen so much crap, we start to see a problem even when one isn't there."

"Mmm." Ms. McCaferty didn't sound convinced.

"You know Tim has ADHD."

"Him and three-quarters of my case-load."

"He's impulsive."

Ms. McCaferty picked what appeared to be a Cheerio out of her hair. "Goes without saying."

The social worker's bangs were stiff with something that had dried all white and flaky—kind of looked like milk.

"What did you do?" Stella asked.

"I said Dean Luchetti wasn't his dad." The woman frowned at the Cheerio. "Tim dumped his breakfast on my head."

Stella thought of Jeremy Janquist. "You got off lucky."

"How is he doing in school?" Ms. Mc-Caferty asked. "May I see his file?"

"Do you have to?"

Ms. McCaferty didn't bother to answer. Stella retrieved the file.

Several minutes passed while the social worker's gaze wandered over the list of offenses. "Doesn't seem like he's adjusting well to me."

"He did those things on purpose."

"I didn't think his fist met another child's stomach by accident."

"Actually you'd be surprised—" Stella broke off at the social worker's get-back-to-the-point glare. "My theory is that Tim was trying to get sent to the office because he thought I needed help in this job. So he was trying to help me adjust, rather than not adjusting himself."

"Compassion is good," the woman said. "His grades are adequate. Improving, even."

"And he hasn't been in the office for several weeks."

Ms. McCaferty handed Stella the file. "That's encouraging."

"Tim *is* adjusting well, and he's bonded with this family. It would be a tragedy to take him away."

"You think Dean Luchetti is good father material?"

"The best."

"What about the bars, the dates? I had a report that he's been in restaurants nearly every night, with different women each time."

Stella had no right to be disappointed, but she was. Before a more disturbing thought hit her.

"Who gave you a report like that?"

"Anonymous tip."

Stella had a feeling she knew who "anonymous" was. She was going to wring her father's neck.

"In my professional opinion," she said, "Tim and Dean belong together."

"Why is that?"

"Dean understands Tim's issues since he has ADHD himself. He handles Tim better than any parent of an ADHD child that I've ever seen, and I've seen quite a few."

"Yes, but doesn't every child deserve a mother?"

"That's what those dates are about," Stella said. "Tim's been setting Dean up in hopes of finding one."

"His father said as much." Ms. McCaferty's face softened. "That's cute."

Stella didn't think so, but she kept her mouth shut.

"You think he'll get married for the sake of the child?"

Stella frowned. "Should he?"

"Judges do look more favorably on two-parent adoptions."

The idea of Dean marrying for Tim bothered Stella. Of course, the idea of him marrying for love was even more disturbing.

"If a judge takes Tim away from Dean he'll be making the mistake of his career. In all my years as an administrator I've never seen a man more capable of being a father."

Ms. McCaferty opened her mouth to comment, but Stella barreled onward. "Do you know how Dean found out he had ADHD?"

"No"

"He took all the tests along with the boy so Tim wouldn't be afraid. No one could understand Tim better."

Ms. McCaferty nodded and made a notation on the file.

"And as for the lack of a mother," Stella continued, "there isn't any lack. He has a wonderful grandmother who lives on the same property. She had six kids in seven years and not one of them is a serial killer."

"Impressive," Ms. McCaferty said dryly. "And she's not insane herself?"

"Not lately," Stella muttered.

"Still, a grandmother isn't a mother."

"He has aunts coming out of his ears. Uncles. Cousins. There's no lack of love on that farm, no lack of female influence in that family."

"Then why is Tim searching for a mother?"

"He's been teased at school. Not having a mom, especially around here—" Stella spread her hands wide. "This isn't the big city. Moms rarely take off and never come back. They don't leave their kids in alleys. They don't name their children Rat."

Since Ms. McCaferty was listening, Stella kept talking. "Tim deserves a break, and I think he's found one at last."

The social worker nodded thoughtfully. "I think you're right."

CHAPTER THIRTEEN

STELLA STOOD. "IT'S been great meeting you."

Ms. McCaferty remained where she was. "I'd like to talk to Tim."

Stella sat back down. "Now?"

"I would have talked to him at the house, but I had hair issues."

"Oh! Well, I can call him down here, but not for too long."

"That's fine."

Stella pressed her intercom. "Laura, can you have Mrs. Neville send Tim Luchetti to the office?"

"I'm sure that won't be a problem since she's done it a hundred times before," Laura muttered.

Stella yanked her finger off the button and smiled wanly at Ms. McCaferty. "He should be right down."

Her intercom buzzed and Stella nearly fell off her chair. "Stella, we've got a problem," Laura said.

"We always do."

The social worker gave her an odd glance, and Stella realized she'd actually sounded happy about it. She couldn't help herself. Stella was a problem solver. She liked fixing things, and fixing kids, or at least their day-to-day troubles, was what she liked to do most of all.

"Tim was sent to the office," Laura continued.

"I know."

"I mean about half an hour ago, but he never arrived. Security didn't see him. I didn't see him. Stella?" Laura took a deep breath, and because Stella had gotten to know her so well over the past few weeks, she sensed rather than heard Laura's panic. "No one's seen him."

"Lock down," Stella snapped. "No one in, no one out. We'll go room to room. Call the police."

"All right. Do you want me to call Dean?"

"No." Stella sighed. "I will."

DEAN HADN'T BEEN ABLE to sit still after the social worker left. He paced, then called his sister.

"Relax," she said. "They need a lot more than that to take the kid away."

"She thought I kicked him."

"You have witnesses who can say you didn't."

"It's just insulting."

"They're paid to be suspicious, Dean. We want them to be. Isn't it better that they question the innocent rather than allow the guilty to go free?"

"You're such a lawyer," Dean muttered.

"Lucky for you that I am."

His sister's words reassured Dean a little, but not enough to allow him to remain inside doing nothing. He fired up his tractor, planning to spread manure on the empty fields. The task might not be pretty, but it was necessary. Following the winter snows, the spring rains, the fields would be rich and ready to plant.

As soon as the engine hummed, the dogs began to bark. They wanted to go along, and since they wouldn't shut up unless they

could, Dean left the tractor idling and released six dogs and one pig, which appeared to think it was a dog, from behind
the fence.

Dean stared at Wilbur, then threw up
his hands. Once the pig had bonded to the
dog, there wasn't much he could do about
it. Brian had a sheep named Ba that thought
it was a rottweiler. No amount of explanations to the contrary had changed her mind.
Ba guarded the house and the people in it.
The ewe was good at it.

An hour later, Dean's mother appeared
at the edge of the field. She lifted her hand,
so he stopped the tractor and got off.

"School called," she announced when he
was still twenty feet away. "Tim's gone."

Dean stared at his mother; his mind
groping for meaning in her words, finding none. "Gone where?"

"No one knows. He was there, then he
wasn't. Stella wants you to—"

Dean didn't wait to hear what Stella
wanted. He ran.

He must have broken every traffic law in
Gainsville; he didn't remember. The panic

in his chest made it hard to breathe; the lack of air made it hard to think.

When he arrived at the school Dean understood why he hadn't been pulled over for speeding. Every emergency vehicle in town was parked in front. There couldn't be an officer left on patrol to pull him over.

He parked in a loading zone and jumped out, frowning at the ambulance in front of him. Had Tim been hurt? Was he lying inside the ambulance right now? Was he conscious? Was he alive? Dean stepped toward the vehicle and someone called his name.

Stella hurried over and took his hand. The gesture seemed the most natural one in the world, and Dean held on tight.

"What happened?" he asked.

"I told your mother—"

"That he was missing, but—" Dean waved his hand at the ambulance, the fire truck, the police cars. "What?"

"As I understand it, volunteer emergency services roll out all the equipment for a 911 call."

"They do?" He had no idea since, thankfully, he'd never had occasion to make one. Yet.

"So I'm told."

"The fire department and paramedics are volunteer," Dean said, "but what's the police department's excuse?"

"Boredom?" Stella shrugged. "We can use the help."

"No sign of him?"

"Sorry." Stella squeezed his hand, then released it. Dean barely managed to keep from clinging. "No."

"What happened?" he repeated.

"As near as I can figure, he was sent to the office—"

"Again?"

"Spitball." She shrugged. "I think he saw Ms. McCaferty—"

Dean stiffened. "She's here? Why?"

"It's common procedure for social workers to come to the school, Dean."

"If you say so."

"I do. Anyway, when I called down to Tim's class so she could talk to him, I found out he'd never made it to the office."

"You searched the school?"

"Top to bottom."

Dean's fingers curled into his palms. "He strolled right out the front door?"

A dad thought his kid was safe at school, but he wasn't. In a modern world, no one was safe anywhere. Dean hated that.

Stella's lips tightened. "Not the front door. That one we watch."

"What about the others?"

"Not watched."

"You ever hear of locking things?"

"Dean, I do know what I'm doing, and even if I didn't, this school has been running smoothly for sixty years."

"Ever lost a kid before?"

"About two or three a year I'm told."

Dean's eyes widened. "How come I never heard about it?"

"Because we always get them back."

"Always?"

She met his gaze. "Yes."

He stuck his hands in his pockets and looked away. "Sorry."

"Don't be. You gave your son to my care, and now he's missing. I'd be a little testy, too. As for the doors—they're all locked, but to keep people on the outside from coming in. We can't lock them so no one can get out."

"Why not?"

Considering the amount and ages of the kids, he was surprised they didn't have a mass exodus daily.

"Can you imagine if we had to run around unlocking every door so we could escape a fire?"

Dean winced. "Oh."

He hadn't thought that out. He was so scared Tim had disappeared forever and he'd never get him back that Dean could barely concentrate.

"He knows how to travel," Dean murmured. "That's how he got here in the first place."

Actually Tim had arrived with Rayne, Aaron's daughter, who'd been thirteen at the time. But Tim wasn't the dimmest bulb in the box. He remembered everything.

"The police checked the bus stop," Stella said.

"He could hitchhike."

Stella frowned. "If anyone from the area

picked him up, wouldn't they bring him right back?"

"It's the people who aren't from the area that I'm worried about."

"Doesn't he know better than to hitch-hike?"

"I've told him, but he's not like the other kids. Tim thinks he's seen it all, and he *has* seen too much. He isn't scared to be on his own." Dean took a deep breath. The kid wasn't scared of anything.

"You should talk to the police chief," Stella said. "He's organizing a search."

Dean choked. "A search?"

Television images from every missing-child case flashed through his mind. Hundreds of people walking through fields or swamps or forests. As the hours turned into days, their faces becoming grimmer.

"We have to do something," Stella said. "We can't just leave him out there. Wherever there is."

"Where's the chief?"

"My office."

Dean followed Stella inside. He figured the school would be in chaos, but it wasn't.

The kids were still in their classes. The teachers were still teaching. He had to give Stella credit. She did seem to know what she was doing.

Stella's office, however, was far from calm. The small area was packed with people. Save one.

"Where's McCaferty?" Dean asked.

"She left right after the police arrived."

Gone to tattle, most likely. This was not going to look good to the judge. Of course, they weren't going to need a judge if they couldn't find his son.

A tall, broad-shouldered man in a tan uniform glanced up from the map he'd been studying at Stella's desk. "You the father?"

The previous police chief had retired last year, and Dean had had no reason to meet the new one. He'd have preferred not to have a reason now.

Stepping forward, Dean held out his hand. "Dean Luchetti."

"Cameron Kelly." The chief's grasp was firm; he shook once and got down to business. "I'm afraid I'm not familiar with the area yet. How about you?"

"Like the back of my hand."

"Great. That'll help. You have any idea where your son might have gone?"

"None."

"Friends?"

"Not really."

Kelly glanced up. "No friends?"

"Tim's new here, too."

A flicker of confusion passed over the man's face. "But you said—"

"Tim came to Gainsville from Las Vegas a few years back. I'm adopting him."

"You think he might head back there?"

"Who knows?"

"Ms. O'Connell had us check the bus stop, straight off." He glanced at her. "Which was a good call."

She smiled. Dean frowned. The two of them were awfully chummy. The surge of jealousy was completely out of place—both because she was Dean's *friend* and because he needed to worry about his son, not Stella's sweet smile at another man.

The chief flicked on his shoulder mike.

"All units keep an eye out for an eight-year-old boy who could be hitchhiking out of town. Check the side roads, as well as the highway."

The new chief was sharp.

"We'll have to fan out from here," he continued. "Ms. O'Connell said he was probably upset, so he might hide, not answer us if we call. We need to look in hidey-hole-type places. Know any?"

"Yeah," Dean answered.

He and his brothers had hidden from their mother often enough.

"You can lead one party. I'll use this—" the chief folded the plot map "—and take another. We'd really benefit from one more person who's familiar with the area."

"That'd be me."

Dean's breath rushed out in relief. "Dad."

"Son." John nodded to the room at large.

Dean was so glad to see his dad he nearly broke down and slobbered on him. In a crisis, there was no one better than John Luchetti. Calm, certain, the rock upon which the Luchetti family was built, he also knew Gainsville and the surrounding area better than anyone.

Dean craned his neck. "Where's Mom?"

"Holding down the fort. We thought Tim might wander home eventually."

"Not if he knows Mom's waiting for him," Dean grumbled.

As a kid Dean had run off a few times, as had all of his brothers. They'd never gone far; they'd always come back. And Eleanor had always been waiting for them. She'd never once slaughtered the fatted calf or treated them like prodigal children. She'd usually grounded them for life and, depending on their age, swatted them on the behind.

"Relax," his dad said. "She'll be so glad to see him, she'll probably smother him with kisses and bake him a cake."

"Pod person," Dean muttered.

"Got that right," John answered.

"Mr. Luchetti." The chief came out from behind Stella's desk to shake John's hand. "Glad to meet you, though I'm sorry it's under these circumstances."

"Let's find the boy, then no one has to be sorry."

John Luchetti always cut to the heart of the matter. When Dean had been a kid, the trait embarrassed him. Lately, Dean appreciated it more and more.

The searchers were divided into three groups. As they headed out, John put his arm around Dean's shoulders and murmured, "We'll find him."

For the first time in a long time, Dean leaned on his father. For the first time in a long time, he needed the comfort and strength only his father could give.

STELLA WATCHED DEAN STRIDE off with several men from town and a single deputy. She wanted to go with him, but she had to stay in her office.

Some of the younger children were upset by all the commotion, and she wouldn't put it past a few of the older ones to make a break for it themselves. Not to mention all the parents who'd started calling the instant they'd heard the news through the amazing powers of the Gainsville grapevine.

She had hopes they'd find Tim nearby and bring him back to school for the afternoon, but those hopes went unrealized. As the day wore on the emergency vehicles left. The searchers made their headquarters at the police station, which only made Stella more nervous.

She didn't hear from Dean, but she didn't expect to. She wasn't his wife; she was the woman who'd lost his son.

"You need to quit sighing." Laura was at the door. "I can hear you out here."

"Sorry. It's just—" Stella lifted her hands, then lowered them.

"I know. He's so little and cute. But I think Tim is a lot tougher than he looks. He'll be all right." Laura smiled. "There's someone here to see you."

"Another parent?"

"Kind of."

"What's a 'kind of' parent?"

"Yours," Laura said, and backed away to let Stella's dad come in.

"Hear you've got trouble," he said, by way of greeting.

"Come to fire me?"

"No. The job offer still stands, as far as I know."

"Then to what do I owe the honor?"

"Your mother wants you to move home."

"I don't think so."

"Well, I asked." He turned toward the door.

"Why did you do it, Father?"

He turned back. "What is it you think I did?"

"Called social services about Tim."

"Is that what this brouhaha is all about? The orphan?"

Stella pursed her lips, then decided not to bother correcting him. What good would it do?

"In a way. I think Tim freaked out when he saw the social worker at school."

"Then he must have something to hide."

Stella snorted. "What does an eight-year-old have to hide?"

"Amazingly nothing from what I could gather."

"You *did* do something!"

"I checked into his background."

Stella wanted to throw a fit, then throw

him out, but she also wanted to know. "What did you find?"

"Not one thing. It's as if the child dropped from the sky. There's never been a single report of anyone looking for a boy that matches his description."

"How strange," Stella murmured.

"I thought so. But if Luchetti wants him, he's got him. No one else seems to care."

His brow wrinkled, as if he found the idea as disturbing as Stella did, but that couldn't be right. Her father had no compassion—especially for anyone named Luchetti.

"If you didn't sic social services on Dean, who did?"

"I doubt the social services department needs anyone to remind them they have a job to do."

"An anonymous source called and said Dean was hanging out in bars every night."

"Is he? I'm not surprised."

Stella ignored the barb. "So you didn't try and have Tim taken away from Dean?"

"Why would I do that when I'd prefer it

if the two of them are wound up in each other and not in you?"

"Me?"

"From what I hear, the child is in your office every day."

"So?"

"And the man is dating everyone he can find in an attempt to get over you."

"What?"

No one knew about her and Dean in this town. Did they?

"That's my theory," her father said. "Maybe one of Luchetti's new girlfriends called social services."

"Why on earth would anyone do that?"

"To get rid of the child." He peered at her closely. "Ready-made families aren't all like *The Brady Bunch*."

"No kidding," Stella muttered.

Could her father be right? Amazingly, his idea had merit.

"What I don't understand," her father continued, "is if Luchetti really cared about you, why was he so easy to scare off?"

Stella experienced a sudden chill, even

though her office was always too hot. "What did you do?"

Her father appeared genuinely surprised. "He never told you? Interesting."

"You tell me," she gritted out between her teeth. "Now."

"I did nothing any father wouldn't do."

"Somehow I doubt that."

"He was trespassing on private property."

For an instant Stella couldn't figure out what he was talking about. Then it struck her with the force of a baseball to the forehead. She even jerked back as if she'd been hit.

"You didn't!"

"Trespassing is a serious offense. I wanted him thrown in jail."

No wonder Dean had broken up with her so abruptly and so painfully.

"Get out," she said.

"Stella, I—"

"Father, if you don't go now, I'm going to say things I might regret, though I doubt

it. You've interfered in my life for the very
last time."

Something in her voice or her face must
have convinced him she was serious, because he went, and he shut the door behind him.

Good. She needed to think.

She could hardly blame Dean for dump-
ing her. He didn't want to end up in jail
and embarrass his family over someone he
didn't even love.

She'd had her heart broken by Dean
Luchetti once, and once had been quite
enough for a single lifetime.

What really disturbed Stella was that
Dean hadn't told her what her father had
done. Not then and not now.

She wanted to ask him why, but she was
afraid he'd tell her that she hadn't been
worth the trouble. And how dumb was it
to be upset that Dean hadn't cared enough
to get thrown into jail over her? He'd been
eighteen and threatened by the most powerful man in town with a charge that, however moronic, would have stuck. Of course
he'd caved. He should have.

In truth, the knowledge of her father's actions only solidified what Dean had told her on that long-ago night. He didn't love her.

CHAPTER FOURTEEN

Night spread across the land. From east to west, shadows crept. The birds stopped singing as the crickets rubbed their legs together.

Tim was so lonely he would have cried if he weren't almost a man. He was so hungry, he'd have eaten a cricket if the very idea didn't make him want to hurl.

He'd eaten garbage in Vegas, but that was people garbage, not bugs. Big difference.

He was about ready to eat garbage again, except he didn't want to go near a house. In Vegas he'd been able to disappear just by moving to a different neighborhood. In Gainsville, everyone knew him on sight, and from the sounds of the shouts all day, they were all looking for him.

He was afraid to come out of his hiding

place. His dad had never laid a hand on him, but he might this time.

Every instinct was tellin' Tim he should leave Gainsville, catch a bus from the next town over, or maybe even two, head to a big city where they'd never be able to catch him.

But if he couldn't be with Dean, if he couldn't be a Luchetti, he didn't even want to *be*. So why run?

He wished he'd thought about that this morning. Now he wasn't quite sure how to go back.

No one would ever find him here. His uncle Bobby had told him about this place, and his uncle Bobby was king of the covert.

Everyone needs a hidey-hole, Tim. You just never know.

The only person Tim had ever brought to the hiding place was Zsa-Zsa, and there was no way she would tell. She mostly said "No!" to everything.

Uncle Bobby was in a sand country, something that ended in *stan*. Tim doubted anyone would be able to call him on the phone and ask him about his hiding place, even if they'd thought to, so Tim was safe here.

For now.

WHEN SCHOOL WAS DONE, Stella couldn't go home. Since the idea of sitting in her silent apartment was unbearable, she sat in her lonely office and tried to work.

At six she called the police chief, at seven the Luchetti farm. There was still no word. Stella wasn't hungry; she wasn't tired. She kept working.

About eight she heard a noise. Figuring it was the janitor, she ignored the sound, until it came again. Then she remembered: the janitor only stayed until seven-thirty when he drove to the middle school and spent the second half of his shift there.

If they had no second-shift security at Gainsville Elementary and the janitor was gone...maybe Tim was back.

Stella jumped to her feet and headed through the darkened outer office and into the shadowy halls. There she experienced her first sense of unease. Maybe she shouldn't investigate alone.

Except no one else was here, and she didn't want Tim to run off before she found him. The prospect of calling Dean and telling him she'd found his son, safe and sound, pushed her forward, down one shadowy corridor after another.

She glanced inside the door of every classroom, but she didn't detect a single movement. Was she imagining things?

The scuff of a shoe made Stella still, then listen. Someone stood just around the next corner, waiting in the second-grade hallway, listening for her as she was listening for him.

Stella took one step backward and stopped.

I will not be afraid for the rest of my life.

The words drifted through her mind and strengthened her resolve. She could not continue to be terrified of the dark, of shadows, of the unknown. But she wasn't stupid, either.

Stella ducked into the nearest classroom, felt around in the utility closet, filtering through the playground items until she found what she needed.

Her fingers closed around cool metal, and she slid back into the hall. When in doubt, a baseball bat could be very empowering.

"Who's there?" she called, proud of her steady, firm voice.

She lifted her arms, tightened her hands. A shadow lengthened, grew and took the shape of a man.

Stella could barely breathe her heart pounded so hard. But instead of allowing the fear to overtake her, she fought against it, refusing to run.

"Don't move," she said.

The man stopped and slowly lifted his hands into the air, as if she held a gun. "You plan to play ball with my head?"

"Dean."

Stella deflated—all the air rushed out, her arms were suddenly too wobbly to hold up the bat. Her heart beat even faster, and she was tempted to sit, right on the floor.

"What are you doing here?" Stella demanded. "I nearly smacked you in the teeth."

He came closer, and she caught that scent

that was uniquely his—fresh grass, summer sun, man—before he gently pried the bat from her fingers.

"I thought Tim might have doubled back. Best place to hide is a place that's already been searched."

"Where'd you learn that?"

"Bobby Luchetti, super-secret soldier school."

"Really? And does Tim know this, too?"

"Tim was number one in the class. He and Bobby are buddies."

An idea entered Stella's head with a near audible pop. "Did Bobby have a hiding place when he was a kid?"

"I'm sure he did, but he never told me." Dean took Stella's arm and led her toward the front of the school. "When we were kids, most of my brothers were usually hiding from me."

"Why?"

"I was a pain."

"No!" she said in mock surprise.

His smile was a shadow of the one she adored. They needed to find that child—for everyone's sake.

"Why are you here?" he asked.

"There's always work to do."

"No play?"

"Not much. And not tonight. I would have liked to help search, but you were already out, and I don't remember the area well enough to go on my own."

Dean paused in the lobby. The light from her office shone just brightly enough so she could see his face. He was tired, and he was scared. He was also the most handsome man she knew, probably because she loved him so much.

Unthinkingly Stella lifted her hand and cupped Dean's cheek. "You'll find him," she whispered.

"I hope so." He tilted his head, increasing the pressure of his face against her palm.

He captured her hand and in a quick, surprising movement placed a kiss to the center. She shuddered with a reaction she tried to disguise. Now was not the time. She wasn't certain there would ever be a time for them again.

"Sooner or later, you'll have to tell me."

"What?" Startled, she fixed her gaze on his.

"Jumping at shadows. Carrying around baseball bats. Dark places. Small spaces."

"I told you I had a problem working."

"There's more to it than that."

He was too intuitive. Always had been.

"The things I've been imagining, Stella," he murmured. "You're giving me nightmares."

Her heart stuttered again. She hadn't thought past keeping her secret. She should have realized that the lack of information would only lead Dean to believe the worst.

"I didn't mean to upset you," she said.

"Then you'll tell me?"

"Yes. But not now."

"No. Right now I need your help."

"Help?" Her brain wasn't working so well. First she'd been terrified, then relieved, then touched. Her mind was mush.

"Help me find Tim."

"Oh." She yanked her hand away and shoved the still-tingling appendage behind her back. "Of course."

"He isn't here," Dean said.

"You're sure."

"No. But if he is, he's safe, at least. Let's look in places where he wouldn't be safe if we left him there too long."

"Like where?"

Dean sighed. "I don't know."

"You're sure he's still in town?"

"Not really. I'd like to wring that social worker's neck for scaring him."

"She never even got near Tim. He's awfully nervous for an eight-year-old."

"He has good reason to be."

"True." And she'd visited the same glass house far too often to throw any stones.

Dean's pocket started ringing, making both of them jump. He yanked the cell phone out and barked "Yeah" into the receiver.

Stella smiled as the memories flowed. Dean had always answered the phone with a similar lack of charm, but she'd always found his James Dean behavior amazingly charming.

"Kim? What?" Dean's face was stark in the half light. He appeared older. Had he aged that much today, or had she just not noticed he'd aged at all until now?

"Calm down," he ordered.

Stella frowned. What could have upset Kim that much?

STELLA'S STRICKEN FACE made Dean realize he was scaring her. He shook his head, and when she collapsed onto the floor, he dropped the phone altogether and went to the ground with her.

"Stella!"

"Is Tim—"

"No!" She'd interpreted his negative shake as very bad news. "I mean, I don't know. He hasn't been found. Kim thinks Zsa-Zsa might know something."

"Isn't she a little young?"

He shrugged. "Kids know stuff."

"Dean? Dean!" Kim's voice came through the dropped cell phone, muffled, both scared and furious.

"Sorry," Dean snapped, and crawled across the floor on his hands and knees to retrieve it.

"What are you playing at?" Kim snapped. "I think we might be on to something here."

"Just tell me what Zsa-Zsa said."

"Did I hear you say Stella?"

"Kim, focus," Dean muttered. "I'm at the school. Stella's here, but my son isn't."

"Okay. Relax." Kim followed her own advice and took a deep breath. "Zsa-Zsa was jibber-jabbering. You know how she does?"

Dean ground his teeth together and said nothing. Stella inched closer, and the scent of her shampoo washed over him. Apples—both tangy and sweet—she smelled exactly the same today as she had all those years ago.

Stella set her hand on his shoulder, and her touch calmed him. It always had.

"We went for a walk," his sister continued. "Through the back field to the trees near the creek. There's a hill where something made a den—fox, coyote, maybe. Zsa-Zsa crawled right in there shouting, 'Timmy, play.' I dragged her out by her ankles and took a look, but it's empty and no one's been there that I can see."

"And this helps me how?"

"I was thinking that the water winds through the pasture where dad keeps Herby."

Dean's blood seemed to curdle. Herby was the meanest Black Angus bull east of the Mississippi. Not that any of them were exactly huggable.

Tim had nearly gotten stomped by Herby the first day he'd come to the farm. Dean had saved him, earning Tim's everlasting love. As a result, Tim knew better than to go anywhere near Herby. Then again, Tim knew better than to run away.

Dean got to his feet, absently tugging Stella to hers along with him.

"When we were kids there was a similar den dug into the creek bank near there," Kim said. "Bobby was always crawling inside. I wasn't supposed to tell anyone, but I think it's safe to say Bobby couldn't fit inside anymore."

"But Tim could."

"Exactly."

"I'm on my way."

"You want me to call Dad?"

"No. The less commotion, the better."

Herby hated commotion.

Dean hit the off button and headed for the front door.

"Wait!" Stella hurried after him. "What did Kim say?"

"Tim might be in an old animal den near the creek."

"I'll go with you."

"No!" Dean swung around, fear making him speak more loudly than he had since Tim had come into his life.

Stella took a step back, and he muttered beneath his breath.

"Sorry," he said. "I didn't mean to scare you."

"I'm not scared." She lifted her chin. "Not of you."

He was glad, but he didn't have time to get all warm and fuzzy about it. "Our bull's in that field. I don't want you near him."

"But Tim can be?"

"No. Which is why I need to get there."

He started for the door; she was right on his heels.

"Stella!" he shouted, and stopped.

She stopped, too. "You sound like Marlon Brando."

"Thanks. Stay here. I'll call you as soon as I check this out."

"I'll only follow in my car."

Dean muttered again.

"I'll stay in the truck," she promised, "but I have to go, Dean. I'm too worried not to."

"Fine," he ground out. They didn't have any more time.

The trip to the farm was quiet. Dean was too upset to talk. Stella appeared in the same boat. He wheeled his pickup onto a gravel road that led to the backfield. As they bumped along, he gritted his teeth so he wouldn't bite his tongue when he hit a particularly bad rut.

Reaching the gate, he put the vehicle into Park and shut off the engine. "I'll be right back."

The key for the gate was on his key ring. He unlocked it, went through and pulled the wooden structure shut behind him, flicking the catch but not reattaching the padlock. If he had to exit in a hurry, he'd rather not be fiddling with a key, or climbing the fence with a bull on his tail.

The field was illuminated by a three-quarter moon, enabling Dean to cross without benefit of a flashlight. He detected no bull-shaped shadows, heard not a tinkle of the bell on Herby's collar, which had been placed there to warn the unwary of his approach.

In no time at all, Dean reached the creek, splashed across the thigh-deep water, crouched in front of a five-foot-wide hole and murmured, "Tim?"

A shadow moved. Nothing growled, or snarled or hissed; nothing spoke, either.

"Tim? Answer me!"

Silence settled over the field. All Dean could hear was the rasp of his own panicked breathing. Then into the stillness fell the sound of a tinkling bell, and a soft voice drifted out of the hole.

"Uh-oh."

STELLA SAW THE PLODDING shadow before she heard the *ring-a-ding-ding*. At first she thought a train was coming, and somewhere in the distance, a crossing signal was clanging. Then she realized the sound was closer, softer, much more deadly.

The bell was on the bull, and it was headed straight for the trees where Dean had disappeared.

Stella wanted to call 911 but Dean had taken the cell phone, and she'd left hers in the office along with her purse. Really, what could emergency services do, anyway? By the time they got here—

She didn't want to think about it.

Stella got out of the truck. The chill of the night pressed against her skin, making her shiver—or maybe it was just the terror.

Should she shout for Dean? Or would that only make the bull mad, or perhaps madder? From what she could recall of bulls, they were pretty much mad all the time for no reason at all.

Stella approached the gate, bit her lip, wrung her hands.

"Oh, that's helping," she muttered.

The bull stopped its progress toward the water and slowly swung its head toward her. Something huge and unwieldy hung from his nose—and not a great big bull-size booger, either. More like a two-by-four.

"What's up with that?"

At the sound of her voice, the bull turned and took a few steps in Stella's direction, so she began to talk about anything she could think of. Her job, both in Gainsville and L.A. Her apartments in the same places. Kids she'd known. Troubles she'd solved and those she hadn't.

How long could she keep this up? Did she expect Dean to slink around the edge of the field while she kept the bull distracted? He could, if he knew what she was doing.

Maybe she should take his truck and go for help, but she couldn't bring herself to leave him.

Just when she thought she couldn't chatter any longer, Tim's voice erupted from the trees. Joy filled Stella, until the bull began to plod in that direction.

"Hey!" she exclaimed, but he was bored with her and didn't even pause.

Panic gripped Stella. Dean had to know the bull was coming—the bell around his neck tinkled in a syncopated rhythm with the animal's steps. The bull had moved so close to the trees he now blended into them.

She racked her mind for a way to make him turn away from the man and the boy. She could only think of one.

Stepping forward, Stella rattled the fence. Nothing happened.

She lifted the latch and shut it again. Same reaction. This side of beef was a lot smarter than she'd thought.

Stella squinted against the night, but she couldn't see even a hint of the bull amid the hazier outlines of the trees. Taking a deep breath, Stella lifted the latch and slid the gate wide open.

Ting-ting, ting-ting, ting-ting.

The bell was swinging, but which way was it moving?

The moon had gone beneath a stray cloud, dousing the field in even deeper shadow. Moving forward, Stella tried to catch a glimpse of something.

The bull burst out of the darkness, two-by-four swaying wildly, the bell clanging violently. He was much closer than Stella ever would have imagined, and she stumbled backward, dragging at the gate, which suddenly refused to budge.

CHAPTER FIFTEEN

Tim was so glad his dad had shown up, he almost jumped out of the hidey-hole and into his arms, then he heard Herby's bell. Usually the bull stayed on the other side of the field, and when he came to the creek for a drink, Tim always heard him long before he got there so he could skedaddle back into the hole. But now his dad stood out in the wide open for any old bull to see.

"We gotta get out of here," Tim said.

"Come on."

"You aren't mad, are ya?"

"Tim."

"'Cause I can explain."

"You always can. Let's do this when we aren't running for our lives, okay?"

"'Kay!" Tim announced, and jumped into Dean's arms.

Tim must have talked a little too loud

since Dad winced and glanced over his shoulder. His whole body tensed. "Get back in there."

"No!" Tim clung to his dad like a monkey, wrapping his arms around Dean's neck and his legs around Dean's waist.

"Tim, you'll be safe in the hole."

"And you'll be dead out here."

"Aw, thanks."

"You will."

In the distance, Tim heard a woman's shout. "Who's that?"

"Ms. O'Connell." His dad tilted his head. "She's talking to Herby, and he's listening." He set Tim on the ground. "Now's our chance, kid. Let's skirt the fence. Keep near me and keep quiet."

"You wanna walk through the field?" Tim asked, shocked.

"How else do we get out of here?"

"The shortcut."

His dad's eyes narrowed. "What shortcut?"

"You think I walked through Herby's field? I'd never. I ain't that dumb."

"But I am," Dad muttered.

"You're not dumb!"

"Keep it down!" Dean said in a voice Tim couldn't quite figure. He sounded like he wanted to laugh and cry at the same time.

"Show me the shortcut, kid." He glanced behind him as the bell started ringing again. "And hurry."

THE SHORTCUT TURNED OUT to be a sprung section of the barbwire fence that kept Herby out of a neighbor's alfalfa field. Although it was big enough for an eight-year-old, Dean scraped his back good when he squeezed through. Luckily, there was no way Herby could manage it.

"This is trespassing," Dean pointed out.

"Better that than cutting through Herby's field. Dad, what were you thinking?"

"I wouldn't be worrying about me if I were you."

Tim hunched his shoulders as they skirted the safe side of the fence.

Dean opened his mouth to read his son the riot act, but Herby's bell began to ring like wind chimes in a tornado. He glanced up and saw the bull charging toward the fence. Herby only charged liked that at a person, and the only other person here was—

Dean began to run. He slid around the corner fence post and saw Stella tugging on the gate.

"Stay back!" he ordered Tim, sensing rather than seeing his son stop.

Time slowed. Dean ran through air as thick as potato soup. His lungs ached with the effort of every single breath.

Stella yanked so hard on the gate, her high heels skidded in the mud, and she fell on one knee, but she scrambled up and kept trying.

"Get in the car!" he shouted.

She shook her head and kept yanking.

Herby's bell dinged in merry contrast to the thunder of his hooves, which jarred the ground. Dean launched his body across the few remaining feet.

There was no time to shove Stella out of the way. Instead, Dean grabbed the gate and tugged. The gate swung shut so fast, Stella's feet came off the ground.

Dean slammed the latch home, just as Herby slammed into the other side. The entire fence shook, and Stella fell with a thud and a grunt.

Dean secured the lock. Herby continued to pound his stupid head against the gate, his two-by-four smashing against it, as well, creating quite a racket.

Stella continued to sit on the ground, legs straight out, her skirt hiked to mid-thigh. If Dean wasn't so scared, he might admire that. As it was, he could barely breathe, and he wanted to punch something. He was getting too old for this.

"What were you doing?" Dean shouted.

"Saving you!" she shouted back, scrambling to her feet, smearing mud all over her suit, her panty hose and her hands in the process.

"I wasn't even in there anymore."

"I didn't know that," she said. "I thought you were dead."

"So did I."

"Don't ever do that again."

"No problem."

As they shouted at each other, they'd gotten closer and closer until they were nose to nose. So he kissed her.

Amazingly, the kiss made Dean feel a whole lot calmer, and then again it didn't.

Stella clung to him, fingers clutching his shoulders. The world fell away, and it became only the two of them, the way it used to be.

Her lips were soft; she tasted exactly the same. Youth, energy, passion—a lifetime ago, yet he remembered everything as if he'd kissed her only yesterday.

Thunder rumbled; the first trace of a storm arrived in the brush of rain against his cheeks.

"Dad?"

Dean yanked his mouth from Stella's. Her eyes were still closed, her expression dreamy, her lips still wet from his.

Dean took a giant step back.

Stella's eyes snapped open, and the dreamy expression fled. She glanced at Tim and groaned, putting her hand to her forehead, leaving a trail of mud behind.

Dean turned to his son, his mind scrambling for an explanation as to why he was kissing the principal. But all speech stopped at the grin on Tim's face.

"What?" Dean asked.

"I didn't say nothin'." Tim ran to the pickup and climbed inside.

"I'm sorry," Stella murmured. "The bull was headed for you. I tried everything I could think of to entice him in my direction, but the only thing that worked was opening the gate, then it wouldn't shut."

Dean sighed. Stella wasn't a farm girl, and she never would be. She'd done the best she could.

"Everything worked out okay," he said.

"So we'll just forget it ever happened?"

He met her gaze. "I doubt that."

WAS HE TALKING ABOUT THE bull or the kiss? Stella was afraid to ask.

Why had he kissed her? Heat of the moment? But that hadn't felt like a heat-of-the-moment kiss. It had felt like a promise of things to come. Dean's kisses always had.

Stella followed him to the truck, climbed in on the passenger side as he climbed behind the wheel. Tim bounced between them, kept from hitting the ceiling by the seat belt across his skinny chest.

"I'm in big trouble, aren't I?" He turned doleful blue eyes in her direction.

"Yep."

"Detention?"

"We'll discuss it."

"How about a suspension?"

Stella slid her gaze toward Dean, and he smirked.

"I don't think so," she said.

"Why not?"

"You think I'm going to give you more days off? That seems like a reward to me."

"Rats," he muttered, glancing at Dean suspiciously.

Dean started the truck and didn't comment.

"What about the social lady?"

"What about her?" Stella asked.

His lower lip trembled. "Is she comin' to take me away?"

Stella and Dean exchanged another glance. "Is that what you thought?"

Tim nodded, eyes shimmering with tears.

Stella put her arm around him. He leaned into her as far as his seat belt would allow.

"I'd never let anyone who wasn't family take you away, Tim. What kind of principal would I be?"

"A bad one?"

"Exactly. I might be new at this particular brand of principal-ing, but I don't think I'm bad at it."

"No. You're gettin' pretty good."

A warm glow began in Stella's stomach, right below the blotch of something brown that she really, really hoped was mud. Tim snuggled close to her side, and the glow got even stronger as Dean pointed the pickup toward home.

Stella frowned. Dean's home. Not hers.

Just because the three of them were all cozy in the truck—Tim getting heavier and heavier against Stella's hip as he dozed— didn't mean she should start dreaming that they were a family. She couldn't.

Dean turned into the lane that led to his parents' house, just as the sky opened and the rain tumbled down.

"I'll drop Tim off with my parents,"

Dean said, "then take you back to your car."

Stella had forgotten she'd come with him from work, and while she hadn't driven her still-rented vehicle the few blocks to school, she *had* left her purse, complete with the keys to her apartment, in her office. She nodded and hugged Tim closer when Dean wasn't looking.

"Mommy," he murmured, and her heart stuttered. Because the idea of being Tim's mommy was far too appealing to a woman who had never had such an idea before.

Dean stopped the truck in front of the farmhouse. Before he even opened his door, his parents appeared on the porch. Dean leaned back in, unhooking Tim's seat belt and pulling the boy into his arms.

Tim mumbled again, but this time the words weren't coherent. As Dean backed out of the cab, their eyes met and she knew he'd heard Tim call her "Mommy," she just wasn't sure what he thought about it.

"I'll be right back," he said, then kicked the door shut.

Mrs. Luchetti cried out at the sight of

Tim in Dean's arms and rushed into the rain, her husband right behind her. Dean jerked his head, indicating they should go into the house.

The three of them disappeared inside, and Stella was left alone. The night had been cool before the rain, now it was downright uncomfortable. The mud—or whatever—that had been ground into her suit, her legs, her feet had dried and begun to flake all over Dean's previously pristine cab. She was miserable.

A door slammed. Stella glanced up as Dean raced from the house to the truck.

The rain had plastered his T-shirt to his upper body, outlining the bulge of his biceps, the ridges of his abdomen. His hair shone in a single flash of lightning, the strands darkened nearly to black by the torrent.

When he opened the door and jumped inside, he brought the scent of rain, sulfur, of night, and suddenly Stella wasn't miserable anymore.

Rivulets ran down his cheeks, and she almost reached out to wipe the drops away.

Her hand even lifted from her lap, but she willed it back, forcing herself to remain still.

"Is Tim all right?"

"He's crashed." Dean shook his head and started the engine again. "Causes an entire day of parental terror, then just closes his eyes and falls away."

"I think that's the definition of *kid*. I saw it in the dictionary." Dean snorted and she smiled. "He had a busy day."

"We all did." He backed up and swung the truck onto the gravel lane that led to the highway. "Do you mind if I stop at my place and check the dogs? My parents could do it, but I want them to stay with Tim."

"No problem."

He turned into the driveway that led to the cottage.

"Aren't the dogs outside?"

"Yeah."

"So what needs checking?"

"Thunder can make dogs nuts. I don't want them to hurt themselves trying to get out from behind the fence, and I'm not sure how Cubby will react. Could make him gun-shy if he can't escape the sound. They should all be inside the barn."

Dean parked right next to the porch steps. "You want something to drink?"

"Definitely."

His lips quirked. "Come on in and I'll set you up, then take care of the animals."

Stella threw open the door, and rain speckled her face. Bracing herself, she hopped out, and moments later was seated at Dean's kitchen table, her hands curled around a coffee mug.

Dean took a long, long swallow. At her raised eyebrows he shrugged. "I need to warm up."

"Me, too."

One of the dogs gave a tentative yelp.

"I'd better take care of them," he said. "Why don't you sit in the living room until I get back?"

"I'm flaking mud all over your floor. I better stay here."

Dean opened his mouth as if to say something else, then snapped it shut and left.

Stella sipped the coffee. She hadn't realized how cold she was until the liquid warmed her belly and began to spread outward. She also hadn't realized how empty her stomach was until two slugs made her nauseous.

She stood and wobbled on her heels. They were encrusted in mud, so she kicked them off, then scowled at the huge runs that marred both legs of her panty hose. She sat and stripped the ruined hose free, tossing them into the trash. The air felt lovely on her heated skin.

Stella took another sip of coffee, then removed her jacket. Her silvery-blue shirt shimmered, cooling the sweat that had sprung up under her arms. She lifted the window over the sink, and the rain-scented breeze blew in, coating her face in a dewy mist.

The back door opened, and she spun around. A little dizzy, half dressed and completely, totally still in love with him, she smiled at the sight of Dean.

She meant to tell him…she wasn't sure what. Something nice, she was certain.

Something adult, nonchalant and unrelated to the turmoil that had been raging inside of her since he'd walked back into her life. But what came out of her mouth instead was: "My father told me he threatened you."

Dean's only reaction was a slight narrowing of his eyes before he slammed the door behind him. He crossed the short distance to the table and poured himself another coffee, but instead of drinking it, he stared into the depths of the mug.

His once-white T-shirt was streaked with dirt, sodden and molded to his body. His hair was damp and slicked back from his face; his chin was darkened with stubble. Marlon Brando and James Dean all rolled into one.

Stella moved across the room and took another healthy slug of coffee.

In for a penny, in for a pound.

"What I can't figure out is why *you* didn't tell me."

DEAN MADE AN IMPATIENT sound and stalked over to shut the window above the sink.

Rain was streaming in. Not that it mattered, since the water just slid down the drain. But he needed something to do other than clasp them around her father's throat.

"None of that matters anymore." He leaned against the counter, afraid to look at her, afraid she'd know how very much it did matter.

Then. Now. Always.

"You should have told me. We would have worked it out."

"I don't know how. Besides…" He took a deep breath and decided to tell her the truth. Maybe that one truth would keep her from discovering any other. "I didn't break up with you because of your dad's asinine threat."

"No?" She didn't sound convinced.

"Stella, he made it the day after he caught us kissing in your kitchen."

He watched understanding spread over her pretty face. "That was before school was even out. All summer we—"

"Exactly. We spent almost every day together by the time I told you I didn't love you."

She flinched, and he felt like a jerk all over again, probably because he was.

"I couldn't have cared less about his threat. Trespassing? Really?"

All I cared about was you.

The words drifted through Dean's mind, but he ignored them. What purpose would be served by telling her such a thing?

"That's why we had to sneak around," she murmured.

"That, and it was exciting. Didn't you think so?"

Her gaze flicked to his. "I thought everything about you was exciting."

Dean had to grasp the countertop until his hands ached to keep from reaching for her. She'd always made him feel ten feet tall. In Stella's eyes he'd never been a loser. But over the years her opinion would have changed, which was why he'd had to make her leave.

He had to make her leave again—before they both did or said something they'd regret.

"You thought dating a moron was exciting?" he murmured.

Her lips tightened. "We didn't date, and who called you a moron?"

"Who didn't?"

"Me."

Silence followed her quiet statement. Dean had nothing to say.

"You weren't stupid, Dean. Not then and not now. You had trouble paying attention and there was a reason for it. One you couldn't help. You're probably brighter than three-quarters of this town."

He knew that now, but the scars of childhood remained. He tried not to reveal they were there; he wanted to set a good example for Tim. But deep down, where such things were hard if not impossible to change, Dean often felt stupid.

"I am who I am," he said, "and I'm doing exactly what I always wanted to. I have no complaints."

Except in the lonely darkness of every single night.

Stella stared at Dean, and he didn't like the expression in her eyes. She was thinking, and she was very good at it.

"I'll drive you home," he said quickly. "You're kind of a mess."

"You said all that to make me leave," she murmured softly, slowly, her voice seeming to awaken, even as her thoughts did. "You wanted me to go to college, to live my dream."

Dean stared at her warily. She seemed kind of angry.

"That wasn't your choice to make. Maybe I'd have been happier here with you."

"I doubt that."

"You said you didn't love me, Dean!" She threw up her hands and began to pace the small confines of the room. "Do you know what that does to a girl? I gave you my heart, and you tossed it back in my face."

"I did it for your own good."

"Oh, well that's okay, then." She stopped pacing and whirled toward him. "Was it your idea or my father's?"

"What?"

"Did my father tell you to dump me?

That the only way to make me leave was to break my heart?"

"I never spoke to your father again after the night he threatened me. There was no reason to."

"So you lied to me all by yourself. I'm not sure if that makes me feel better or worse."

"Stella—" Dean took a step forward.

"You stay over there." She pointed to the sink. "I can't think when you're close to me."

Which only made two of them. Dean leaned against the counter once more.

"I cried for months," she whispered. "I wanted to die."

"I wasn't worth it."

"Shut up," she said, the calm of her voice a contrast to the storm in her eyes. "You were to me."

"It was for the best. Look what you did."

"You talk like I cured cancer. Or ran for president. I became an educator."

"In my book, that's everything. You teach kids, Stella. You help people. What's more important than that?" He shook his head. "You say your dad's a fool, but subconsciously you believe everything he says."

"I never believed you were worthless."

"But I did."

"Aren't we a pair?" Stella asked. "Both haunted by a past we really need to get over."

"What haunts you, Stella?"

Her gaze met his. "I told you—or maybe you told me. Can't seem to stop wanting Daddy's approval, even though I know it'll never come."

Dean took a step closer. He'd been patient; he'd waited for her to tell him the truth, but his patience was at an end. Her eyes still held shadows; he wanted them gone, or at least he wanted to know what had put them there.

"You know that's not what I meant," he said softly.

"I know." Her voice was equally quiet. She sat at the kitchen table and stared into her mug of coffee. "I'm not sure if I can do this."

"Of course you can." Dean took a seat

on the other side of the table, then he held his breath, waiting, hoping, praying that Stella would trust him at last.

CHAPTER SIXTEEN

"I'VE NEVER TOLD ANYONE," she said. "Not everything."

"Maybe that's the problem."

"Maybe."

Having Dean here, so warm and big and strong, made her feel safe. For the first time since "the incident" she wanted to talk about what had happened, and maybe Dean was right; maybe part of her problem had been that she hadn't.

"Last spring I stayed late at school," Stella began, "which I did a lot. The high school I was in charge of had three thousand students."

Dean's eyes widened. "Gainsville has about three thousand people."

"Who all behave much better than high school students in L.A."

"I bet," he mumbled.

"A big part of my job was paperwork. The other part was discipline. The buck stopped with me. From my office, problem children were sent directly to jail."

"I take it most offenses went beyond cutting classes and starting food fights."

"More like cutting people and starting riots. Most students didn't take an expulsion personally. They didn't really want to be there, anyway."

"Most of them," Dean repeated. "What about the others?"

"A lot of kids *did* want to be in school, but they couldn't control their impulses."

"What kind of impulses?"

"Drugs, pathological violence."

Dean took her hand, and she let him. "Why did you do it?"

"I was good at my job, and I loved it."

"How could you?"

"Some of those kids had a chance. I gave them a place they could learn. For some, school was the only safe haven they'd ever had, and I wanted to make sure it stayed that way. Kids deserve a safe school."

Dean's fingers tightened on hers. This

was nice, talking in the night as the rain brushed the windowpanes, holding hands.

"So…" Dean said, and the collar of his shirt shifted, revealing the long, brown line of his throat.

"Which little jerk hurt you," Dean continued, "and is he dead yet?"

Every speck of romance fled, and Stella yanked her hand from his. "He was sixteen."

"Old enough to know better."

"Maybe," Stella said. In Frank's case she still wasn't sure.

"Hurting a woman is wrong," Dean insisted, "and every male knows it from the day he knows his name."

He sounded so certain, she sighed. In his world, that was true, but in hers, not so much.

"You know some men enjoy hurting women."

"Those aren't men, Stella."

She missed his hand, but she wasn't going to take it back.

"You were working late one night…" he said encouragingly.

"Yes. I didn't realize how late. I was the last one there."

"No security? No janitor?"

"Frank killed the janitor. A nice old man named Mr. Benito. I don't think Frank *meant* to kill him. He hit him too hard."

"And the security guard?"

"Frank hit him, but not too hard."

Thankfully, or Frank Watson would have succeeded in killing her.

"I—" Stella's voice cracked, and she had to swallow a few times before she could go on. Dean said nothing, did nothing, just patiently waited for her to regain control.

Which was nice. It had been a long time since anyone had thought she'd be fine without help.

"I gathered my stuff," she continued, "and I headed for the door to the teachers' parking lot. I had a walkie-talkie, and I tried to raise the security guard. I always had him watch me until I was in the car and on my way. In the end, it didn't help. Frank was already in the building."

"What happened to your security system?"

"Frank was a computer genius."

"He bypassed the alarm?"

Stella nodded. "What a waste."

"You should sue the security provider."

"I meant a waste of talent," Stella said. "Frank could have done so much, if he'd only put his genius to good use."

"Since you're speaking of him in the past tense, I'll assume he's no longer in need of the punch in the nose I had planned for him."

"You don't even know what he did, Dean."

Dean reached out and ran his thumb over her cheekbone. "He put shadows in your eyes. He made you jump when I try to touch you. I hate him for that."

"He was sixteen," she repeated.

"I don't care." His hand fell away. "Now, finish the story. I'm sure the truth has to be less upsetting than anything I've imagined, or at least I hope it is."

"Depends what you imagined."

"I knew something happened in L.A., and that it had to be awful to make you come back here. How awful was it, Stella?"

Suddenly she couldn't find the words.

Stella had been raised in a world without physical violence, and even though she'd entered one where violence was commonplace, she hadn't been prepared for how being hit had made her feel. Sure it hurt, but worse it pained her. Even after the bruises went away, the fear and the degradation remained.

"Was this a random attack? He got in because he could, then you happened to be there?"

"No. He planned the entire thing just for me, which would have gotten him death row if he'd actually succeeded in killing me."

As it was, Frank had gotten death, anyway. Why did she still feel bad about that?

"What could you have done to make him so angry?"

Frank had been angry from birth, but a lot of the kids she dealt with were. There'd been something missing in Frank, something that made him think he could do whatever he wanted and get away with it.

"He was furious because I'd expelled

him for hacking into the grading system and wiping everything out."

Dean raised an eyebrow. "Really?"

"Like I said—genius completely wasted."

"Doesn't sound wasted to me. We used to dream about doing just that at Gainsville High."

"We keep hard copies. His little stunt only meant we had to work overtime to put everything back the way it was before he messed with it."

"So he wasn't being a Good Samaritan, he was just being mean."

"Which is why he got expelled. Frank took offense. He thought I should have praised him. He wanted me to get his computer teacher to raise his grade."

Dean frowned. "This kid sounds like a serious problem. What was he doing in school?"

"Public school." Stella spread her hands. "Couldn't keep him out until he did something wrong."

He stared at her for a long minute. "I think you got me off the subject of Frank."

"I didn't mean to." Stella took a deep breath and went back to the story. "When the security guard didn't answer, I headed for the rear entrance, figuring he'd show up there eventually. Frank knew I left by that door. He waited around a corner and *pow*—" Stella made a jabbing motion with one fist "—out went the lights."

"He punched you?"

"What did you think he did, Dean, gave me a really bad paper cut?"

His eyes narrowed. "And then?"

"When I came to, I was tied up in my office. It was dark, and he was hovering in the shadows, teasing me. He'd loom up out of nowhere, punch or slap me, then disappear."

Which was how she'd gotten so spooked by the shadows of men in the darkness and fast movements any old time.

"He would have killed me," she whispered. "He knew Mr. Benito was dead, and even though he hadn't meant to do it, he also knew that one more death—"

They can't fry me twice, Ms. O'Connell.

"What happened to the security guard?"

"Woke up. Figured Frank was headed for me and came to my office."

"And then?"

She met his eyes. "He hit Frank a little too hard."

DEAN COULD TELL STELLA felt bad about that, but he didn't.

Who'd have guessed he was a vigilante at heart? Probably every one of his high school teachers.

"You came to Gainsville to rest," he murmured.

"Not exactly."

"What exactly."

"Medical leave."

His chest tightened at the thought of what might be wrong with her. He didn't know how to ask.

"Actually, psychiatric leave," she continued.

His chest eased, although mental illness might be worse than anything else.

"Don't you want to know why?" she asked.

"Uh, sure."

Stella rubbed her forehead, then with a sigh, she dropped her hand and blurted, "I couldn't do it."

Dean waited, but she didn't elaborate. "Do what?"

"My job. The bruises went away, but what got them there didn't. Frank was dead, but I saw him everywhere at school."

"And you think there's something wrong with that? If you didn't, Stella, you should have your head examined."

She leaned her elbows on the table, shoulders hunched, and Dean reached for her hand again.

"When you see someone who's dead," she said, "and you think they're coming after you, you can't be the principal of a school."

"You didn't get over being attacked by one of your students quickly enough, so they fired you?"

"A medical leave isn't fired—although if I can't get over my irrational fear—"

"I wouldn't call it irrational."

"My boss does. At any rate, a leave was strongly recommended. The third time they found me hiding under the desk was one time too many."

Dean made a disgusted sound. "What are you going to do?"

"Hope I wake up one morning and all my irrational fears have disappeared?"

"Yeah. That'll happen." Dean considered her for a moment. "I'm no expert, but I think you need a psychiatrist."

"Saw one. Didn't help."

"Is it better for you to avoid the situations that scare you or confront them?"

"That depends."

"On what?"

"Who you listen to. Everyone's got a theory." She squeezed his hand, smiled too brightly, then straightened. "I feel better now that I've finally told someone everything."

"What did you tell me that you didn't tell the psychiatrist?"

If he hadn't been touching her, Dean wouldn't have felt her start. "Or maybe I should ask what didn't you tell me, either?"

She looked away.

"Stella?" Dean's fingers tightened. "What else did he do?"

"Nothing. It was something I did."

"You can tell me."

She took a deep breath, and it shook in the middle, as if she'd been crying for hours. Dean had a feeling she'd been crying silently for months, and the idea made him want to break something, preferably Frank, but that was already done.

"I begged him not to kill me."

She was mortified, and Dean wasn't sure why.

"Big deal," he said. "I'd have been begging like a—like a beggar. There's no shame in that, Stella. Are you nuts?"

"Yes." She stared at him now, her eyes huge and bright. "I thought we'd established that."

He wasn't sure what to say. He didn't want to make her cry. Then she smiled, and his heart went *ba-boom*.

She was teasing, and that she could when she was so sad and lost only made him more fascinated with her now than he'd been fourteen years ago.

"I've been better since I came here," she said.

"Why?"

"I don't know, but—"

"But what?" He rubbed his thumb over hers.

"Why did you kiss me?"

"Which time?" he asked, getting to his feet and taking their empty mugs to the sink.

"A question isn't an answer."

"No?" He turned as her eyes narrowed, and he laughed. "Sorry."

She stood and crossed the short distance separating them. Dean tried to move back, but he was already flush with the counter.

Stopping so close he could smell the rain on her skin, she peered into his face. "Sorry about the kisses?"

"No."

The word slipped out, he wanted to take it back, but it was too late.

Stella put her hand on his arm, and Dean realized in that moment why he'd never married, why he'd barely dated. It had always been her, and he didn't know if he'd ever be able to find anyone else who made him feel the way that she did.

"Did you ever love me?" she murmured.

Something in her voice made him answer. She needed to know the truth, and maybe it was time.

She'd just given him the truth. Though it was a mistake, Dean could do no less for her.

"Yes."

CHAPTER SEVENTEEN

STELLA AWOKE IN THE middle of the night, in a strange bed. For an instant she couldn't remember where she was or why. Then she caught the scent of Dean on the pillow, and it all came rushing back. She had been so tired after the long day that Dean gave her his bed while he took Tim's.

Determination filled her. He'd loved her once, he could love her again.

Her gaze wandered over the room. Plain, sturdy furniture, white sheets, a handmade quilt. The room reflected the nature of the man. He belonged here, and so did she.

She might not know anything about animals or farming, but she knew about love, with him. And to her mind, love trumped everything—her father, her allergies, Dean's fears and insecurities. Now she only had to convince him of that.

Deep in thought, Stella was startled by a creak of a floorboard, and she spun toward the sound. The shadow of a man loomed in the doorway. She waited for the fear, the panic. None came.

She was safe in Dean's house, on his farm, in Gainsville. Going back to L.A. had never seemed like a dumber idea.

"Hey," she murmured. "You okay?"

Dean moved slowly into the room, then sat on the edge of the bed and hung his head. Stella inched closer, wrapped her arms around his waist, laid her cheek against his shoulder.

"Kissing you again was a mistake," he said.

"Didn't feel like a mistake to me."

"Stella—"

"Don't tell me all the reasons you shouldn't have kissed me. There's only one reason I want to hear." She tightened her arms. "Why you did."

He turned, his eyes glittering in the faint light from the hall. He was so beautiful he made her heart ache. He always had.

"I couldn't help myself." Leaning forward, he brushed his lips over hers. "I still can't."

From the way that he touched her, she could swear that he loved her. But she was still too afraid to ask.

"Dean?" she whispered to the darkest part of the night.

"Yes?" His voice was wary. She couldn't blame him.

"Being here with you makes everything all right."

"Go to sleep, Stella," he said, but she heard the smile in his voice as he turned and headed back to Tim's room.

As she drifted off, everything *was* all right for the first time in a lifetime.

OF COURSE, IT DIDN'T LAST.

Stella awoke to the sun shining in her face. She experienced a momentary heart attack at the thought of sleeping right through the tardy bell.

No one would know where she was. Her purse was still in her office. Laura would have a stroke. Right after she called in the marines.

But a quick glance at the clock revealed it was only 6:45 a.m. She had plenty of time, and she smelled coffee.

Since her clothes were probably still in the washing machine, Stella borrowed a robe from the closet, then followed her nose to the kitchen.

Dean didn't hear her approach, so she was given a moment to study him while he leaned against the counter drinking coffee.

His eyes met hers, and every memory passed between them. He smiled.

"Morning," he said. "Coffee?"

"Please."

Stella sat at the table because she didn't know how much longer she could stand and not wobble.

Dean set a mug in front of her, and his forearm brushed her shoulder. Unconsciously she leaned into him. Smiling, he moved away, taking the chair on the opposite side of the table.

"Where are the dogs, Wilbur, Tim?"

"Not here," he said.

A tap interrupted them. They both glanced at the door and froze.

Ms. McCaferty stood on the other side of the screen, eyes wide as she took in the scene in front of her.

Dean half asleep. Stella in his robe.

The social worker's gaze met Stella's, and she scowled as her lips pursed. "No wonder you gave him such a good recommendation."

Ms. McCaferty turned on her heel and stomped away.

Stella looked at Dean. "Who's screwing up whose life now?"

CHAPTER EIGHTEEN

"WHAT ARE YOU TALKING about?" Dean asked.

"I gave you a good recommendation when she came to the school. Now she knows why. Or at least she thinks she knows why."

"Why?"

Exasperation flashed across her face. "Because I spent the night at your house."

He tilted his head. "But nothing happened."

"This isn't funny, Dean. She could really mess things up with the adoption."

"No way," he said, and shoved back his chair. He'd had all he could take of dancing around social services. He meant to end this today.

Stella made a grab for him, but Dean was already out of her reach. He slammed

through the door, and chased Ms. Mc-
Caferty across the yard, catching up to her
in front of her car.

"What's your problem?" he demanded.

She spun around. "Today, it's you."

"What did I do?"

Her gaze flicked over him from head to
foot. "Plenty, from the looks of you."

Dean refused to lower his eyes. He lifted
his chin and stared the woman down. "This
is none of your business."

"We don't give children to gigolos."

Dean choked. That was something he'd
never been called. His brother, Evan, on
the other hand...

"We specifically don't allow people
who—who—"

"People who what?"

Her eyes widened. If it were possible,
steam would have come from her ears.
"People who don't even care where their
child is," she snapped.

"Hold on," he interrupted, steam threat-
ening to pour out of his own ears. "You
think I was with Stella while my son was
lost?"

Uncertainty filtered over Ms. McCaferty's face. "Weren't you?"

"No. Tim is at my parents' house. Sleeping."

"No, he isn't."

Tim stepped out of the cornfield.

"How long have you been there?" Dean demanded.

"Not long."

The corn rustled and Cubby shot out, trailed by Wilbur. Horror spread over Ms. McCaferty's face, but she didn't bolt, even when the doodles and Bear followed.

"Stay!" Dean bellowed, and everyone jumped.

The animals, to a one, sat and stared at Dean, waiting for further commands, Wilbur tilting his head exactly the way that Cubby did.

Even Dean, who'd never been much for barnyard animal pets, thought that was cute. He turned to Ms. McCaferty, who seemed to be the only person in a million unaffected.

Dean took a deep breath, and when he spoke, he was proud of how composed he sounded, despite the raging case of nerves in his belly.

"We found Tim last night," he said. "I should have called to let you know. I'm sorry. Now, what can I do for you this morning?"

Ms. McCaferty stared at him for several seconds, then sighed. "I apologize for jumping to conclusions. Comes from too many years giving people the benefit of the doubt and being burned for it, or having the children in my care hurt because of it. I know I'm overly suspicious and rigid, but I have good reason to be."

"That's understandable," Dean said.

"Thank you." Ms. McCaferty cast a wary glance at the animals and continued. "But I have to tell you, I'm concerned about Tim."

"I'm fine!" Tim shouted.

"Tim!"

The social worker's lips twitched. "A child his age needs a mother."

"I ain't never had one before," Tim announced.

"Which is why you should have one now," she said, without taking her eyes from Dean's. For some reason, her being nice was more disturbing than her being nasty. "I can't give my recommendation for adoption under these circumstances. I'm sorry."

Dean glanced at Stella. "Call Kim."

STELLA WAS ROOTED to the porch, unable to move, barely able to breathe as the answer to all their problems became clear.

"Stella!" Dean said. "You mind?"

She needed to speak up, but she was afraid. She'd said the same things to him before, and he'd thrown them back in her face. But so much more was at stake now than there'd been then.

"You don't need Kim," Stella blurted. "You've got me."

Dean was so focused on Ms. McCaferty, he answered without even glancing her way. "You're a principal, not a lawyer."

Stella came down the steps and crossed the yard, winking at Tim as she went by. His sweet, worried face wrinkled, then smoothed. He might not know what she was going to do, but he trusted her to help.

Knowing that only made her all the more determined to do what needed to be done, regardless of the risk to her heart.

Stopping directly in front of Dean, Stella took his hand. "I'm the woman who loves you."

"Stella, we've been over this—"

"No. You've been over it. You never once asked what I wanted."

"What do you want?"

"All I've ever wanted, Dean, was you."

Silence settled over the yard, broken only by the grumbles and groans from the herd of dogs, and one amazingly dainty snort from Wilbur.

"I can't let you marry me so I can adopt Tim," Dean said. "It wouldn't be right."

"No kidding," Ms. McCaferty muttered.

Stella ignored her. "You said you broke my heart when I was seventeen *because* you loved me. You plan to do the same thing now?"

"Yes."

"Then you still love me."

"Stella—"

"Tell me the truth," she snapped, letting

go of his hand. "Just once in our lives, Dean. Just once."

If he turned her away now, she'd be devastated. She'd never wanted anything as much as she wanted to make a family of three, and then some, with him.

He seemed to struggle, clenching his jaw, his fists, too. Shaking his head as if denying an inner voice, at last he threw up his hands. "I never stopped loving you, Stella, and I never will."

He pulled her into his arms, and as he kissed her, the past and the present merged into one future. Everything *was* going to be all right.

"Marry me?" Dean asked.

"Yes."

"Not just for her." He jerked his head at Ms. McCaferty.

"I know."

And she did know. Dean loved her. He always had. She wanted to tuck that knowledge inside and enjoy it a while, but more people crept out of the cornfield.

"When's the wedding?" Eleanor asked.

Dean squeezed Stella's shoulders and faced his mother. "The sooner the better."

A huge smile appeared on his mom's face and her gaze met Stella's. "Thank you," she said.

"For what?"

"Making him happy again."

"Thank *you*," Stella returned.

"For what?"

"Making him."

"I think I might have had something to do with that," Dean's father murmured.

"Well, thank you, too."

John glanced at his wife.

"Don't," she said. "You'll scare her away."

He snorted. "If she scares that easy, she'll never survive here."

"Dad," Dean began, but his father waved his protest away.

"Knock-knock," John said.

"Oh, I love these!" Stella cried. "Who's there?"

"Teacher."

She smiled. He'd put a lot of thought into this.

"Teacher who?"

"Teacher to go knocking on my door in the middle of the night."

Stella snickered. So did Tim. Dean and his mother groaned.

"At last," John said, "one for my side."

Stella gave Dean a quizzical look.

"Dad tells every new member of this family a knock-knock. Some of us hate them—"

"Like me," his mom stated.

"And others don't," her husband interjected. "Like Tim and Zsa-Zsa."

"And me," Stella said. "Great company I have."

"Got that right." John gave her an awkward hug. "Welcome."

When he released her, there was a tug on Stella's robe.

"You wanna be my mommy?"

Tim's face was so full of hope, Stella went down on her knees. "More than just about anything."

"Yay!" Tim shouted. "I was tryin' real hard to get you two together."

"What are you talking about?" Dean asked.

"I kept gettin' you bad dates." Tim rolled his eyes. "Didn't you notice?"

"Those were *supposed* to be bad dates?"

"Dad. They were all terrible mommy material."

"They were."

"I wanted you to see that the only one worth keepin' was her." Tim threw his arms around Stella's neck and squeezed.

When he released her, Stella kissed his nose and he giggled.

"The mommy quest is done," Tim said. "We're a family."

Dean turned toward Ms. McCaferty, who'd been amazingly silent the entire time. "I hope we'll be a family," he said.

Ms. McCaferty considered Dean, Stella, Tim, Dean's parents, the dogs and the pig, then she threw up her hands. "You win. You're perfect for each other. Now you just have to convince the judge."

"Yippee!" Tim shouted as Ms. McCaferty got into her car and drove away. "I hope she never comes back."

"Ditto," Dean muttered.

"Ditto," Stella echoed.

"So," Tim said, "how fast can I get a sister?"

Stella choked. Dean smacked himself in the forehead. His parents shook their heads and walked into the cornfield.

Tim blinked, all innocent blue eyes and adorable freckles. "Whad I say?"

EPILOGUE

DEAN COULDN'T BELIEVE all the rigmarole necessary to plan even a small wedding. If it wasn't for his mother, he doubted they'd have been able to manage it at all. Once Stella had agreed to accept the position of principal at Gainsville Elementary for the rest of the year, she became busier than ever.

"I want everyone to know how much I love you," he told her every chance he got.

He was embarrassed that he'd denied it for so long, even if it had been for Stella's own good. Or what he thought was her own good. Instead, she'd been miserable for years and so had he.

Opening up about the night of her attack had helped Stella begin to heal. She was still jumpier than he cared for, and her eyes had shadows that might never go away, but she was better. And Dean believed she'd only get better the longer she lived in Gainsville with him and Tim.

The day of their wedding arrived nearly a month after the engagement. They would be married at his parents' house, under a gazebo Dean's brother Evan had built. Every last one of the Luchettis had arrived yesterday. Last night they'd celebrated the best gift of all. Tim's adoption became final.

"I'm a Luchetti forevermore!" he'd shouted, and even the sour-faced judge who'd presided over everything had to smile.

About midafternoon, Brian arrived to drive Dean around the block to the ceremony.

"Walking through the cornfield in tuxedos is not allowed," Brian announced. "Besides, isn't this what a best man is for?"

"Thanks for agreeing to do it."

Dean had been unable to choose between his brothers for the position of best man, and in truth, Brian had always been as close to him as any Luchetti.

"Anytime. Although I think you'll only get married one time. Stella's the woman for you."

"She always has been."

Silence settled over them. It seemed companionable until Brian blurted, "Kim's going to have another baby."

"I thought you were going to wait."

"We didn't."

Dean snorted. "No kidding. Is she mad?"

"She's happy." Brian's forehead creased. "She did say I get to take care of the baby while she works."

Dean thought about it for a second, then shrugged. "That doesn't sound so bad."

"My thoughts exactly."

The yard at the main house was full of pickup trucks in every color. Dean had left his red one there last night. Parked next to it was Colin's black truck, then Evan's silver and Aaron's bright blue. Only Bobby hadn't arrived with one since he'd flown in from Blah-blah-stan, as his wife arrived from Quintana Roo.

"Dad!"

Tim ran out to meet them dressed in a

miniature tuxedo. He already had a splotch of dirt on the knee.

"Gramma says Cubby and Wilbur can't come to the wedding." His lip wobbled.

"Don't even try it, kid. This time I agree with Gramma."

"Rats." Tim kicked the dirt, sending a puff of dust over the already scuffed tip of his black shoes.

"I thought you invited some of your friends from the football team to the party?"

"I did."

"Then what are you whining about?" Dean asked. "Take a hike."

"'Kay!"

"And don't get dirty."

"Right," Tim called over his shoulder with a laugh.

"Go, go, go, go!" Zsa-Zsa twirled around and around on the grass, the blue-and-silver skirt of her cheerleading outfit belling around her legs. She shook her arms in time with the words, jangling the sparkly pom-poms in her hands.

Kim had made good on the threat to buy

her daughter the costume. Now Zsa-Zsa refused to take it off. Somehow that was fitting.

The sound of a car coming down the lane set the dogs penned behind the fence to barking. They stopped at a sharp rebuke from the third-floor window. His mother must be getting dressed.

"Who is it?" Brian asked.

Dean didn't answer as the car stopped, and Stella's parents climbed out.

"Oh," Brian said, and drifted away.

"Sir." Dean nodded stiffly.

George O'Connell returned the nod. His wife, a slim waif of a woman whom Dean had never formally met, gave her husband an elbow in the ribs.

"Ahem." O'Connell cleared his throat. "I came to bury the hatchet."

"In my head?"

"Uh. No. Make the peace." He held out his hand. "For Stella's sake."

Dean was so shocked he didn't take the hand right away and O'Connell kept talking—after his wife stomped on his foot.

"I apologize for how I behaved. I was wrong."

"I wouldn't say that," Dean murmured. "If I found my daughter with a guy like me, I'd have gotten the gun."

O'Connell's lips twitched. "It did cross my mind."

STELLA WAS JUST ABOUT to put on her wedding dress when she glanced out the window, then she ran out of the house.

"Father!"

Everyone glanced in her direction. Dean slapped his hands over his eyes.

"What are you doing?" she asked.

"I'm not supposed to see you before the wedding."

She tugged on his fingers. "You aren't supposed to see me in my dress."

He opened his eyes and smiled at the sight of her in his robe. Ever since that day at his house, she'd refused to give the garment back. It was hers now, and so was he. Or almost.

Stella placed a kiss in the center of Dean's palm. His eyes gleamed. He couldn't wait for the ceremony, and neither could she. But first they had to get through the preparations. Keeping Dean's fingers linked with hers, she faced her father.

"Don't ruin this for me."

"He came to make peace," Dean interjected.

"He did?"

Stella and her father hadn't spoken since the day she'd thrown him out of her office. She didn't regret it. He'd been wrong. But she had wanted to smooth things over since they were going to be living in the same town.

The wedding invitation she'd sent had gone unanswered, and she'd figured any chance at reconciliation had vanished with her angry words. The lack of her parents had been the one shadow on an otherwise crystal-clear horizon.

"Your mother told me I made peace, or I packed my bags," her father said.

Stella glanced at her mother. "You did?"

"I did."

"What got into you?"

"My daughter's going to be with the man

she loves for the rest of her life. I wanted that, too."

Stella turned her attention to her father, who shrugged.

"I have to revert to the man she married or she'll divorce me," her father said, but he was smiling.

"Pod person," she muttered, and Dean snickered.

"You took the principal's job?" her father asked, though as a school-board member, he had to already know the answer.

"George!"

"I just want to congratulate her."

"All right. But be nice." Stella's mother moved off to greet Dean's mom, who had insisted Stella call her Ellie.

"You don't mind that I'm a nose wiper?" Stella couldn't resist asking.

"I doubt you wipe many noses in the principal's office."

"You'd be surprised."

Her father rocked back on his heels.

"What?" she asked, knowing he had something else to say.

"You ever consider being a superintendent?"

Stella tilted her head. "Not until just now."

Her father's smile widened. Tim ran up and tugged on his trousers.

"Are you my grampa?"

Everyone stilled. Stella took a step forward, but Dean put a hand on her arm and shook his head. He was right. Here was the test. Had her father truly changed or was he merely pretending?

He scowled at Tim, chewed his lip, and Tim grinned, exposing his missing teeth. George O'Connell's scowl melted, as did his heart. He lifted Tim into his arms. "I guess I am."

DEAN AND STELLA WERE married in the gazebo with all of the Luchettis and her parents looking on. Stella couldn't have imagined a lovelier wedding or a better present than her father's blessing. Until John and Ellie pulled them aside.

"Here." John handed Dean a long envelope.

"What's this?"

"Wedding gift." Dean's parents shared a smile.

Dean opened the flap, took out legal documents, glanced at them and shook his head. "Dad—"

"It's time."

"What is it?" Stella asked.

"They've given us the farm and the house."

"We'll move into the thresher's cottage next week," Ellie announced.

"Oh, no," Stella protested.

"Oh, yes. I'm getting too old to keep up such a big place, and from the looks of you two, you're going to need more rooms."

Stella smiled. Her mother-in-law had babies on the brain, as did Tim, who had made it his mission to nag her daily for a sister. He called it the sister quest.

"Are you going to be okay living on a farm?" Ellie asked.

"Why wouldn't I be?"

"I thought you were allergic to hay?"

Stella blinked. "I thought I was, too."

However, she hadn't sneezed once since

she'd returned to Gainsville. Maybe she'd grown out of it, as her allergist always insisted she could. If the problem came back, she'd just take a pill. Everyone else did.

Her fear of shadows in the dark had waned. Probably because the darkness now held Dean. With him at her side, she didn't have to be afraid of anything anymore, and knowing she wasn't going back to L.A. didn't hurt, either.

"What about the dogs?" Ellie continued.

Stella's gaze went to the back fence where six of them, plus a pig, stared at the crowd hopefully. She'd been here so much in the past month, they'd kind of grown on her. In fact, when she told them to be quiet, sometimes they even listened.

"I think I'm going to be all right," Stella murmured.

"I think we both are." Dean put his arm around her shoulders and kissed her forehead.

The rest of the day was the best of Stella's life. She liked all of Dean's brothers, but then she always had, and each of their wives was perfect for the Luchetti they'd married.

Stella gazed at the group. Everyone was happy, even her parents. Thank God for huge miracles.

Her eyes turned to Dean. And speaking of miracles…

Stella now had her own miracle—she married the man of her dreams and she had a little boy who called her Mom every chance he got.

* * * * *

REQUEST YOUR FREE BOOKS!
2 FREE WHOLESOME ROMANCE NOVELS
IN LARGER PRINT
PLUS 2
FREE
MYSTERY GIFTS

HEARTWARMING™

Wholesome, tender romances

YES! Please send me 2 FREE Harlequin® Heartwarming Larger Print novels and my 2 FREE mystery gifts (gifts worth about $10). After receiving them, if I don't wish to receive any more books, I can return the shipping statement marked "cancel." If I don't cancel, I will receive 3 brand-new larger-print novels every month and be billed just $4.74 per book in the U.S. or $5.74 per book in Canada. That's a savings of at least 21% off the cover price. It's quite a bargain! Shipping and handling is just 50¢ per book in the U.S. and 75¢ per book in Canada.* I understand that accepting the 2 free books and gifts places me under no obligation to buy anything. I can always return a shipment and cancel at any time. Even if I never buy another book, the two free books and gifts are mine to keep forever.

160/360 IDN FV7S

Name	(PLEASE PRINT)

Address	Apt. #

City	State/Prov.	Zip/Postal Code

Signature (if under 18, a parent or guardian must sign)

Mail to the **Reader Service:**
IN U.S.A.: P.O. Box 1867, Buffalo, NY 14240-1867
IN CANADA: P.O. Box 609, Fort Erie, Ontario L2A 5X3

Not valid for current subscribers to Harlequin Heartwarming Larger-Print books.

* Terms and prices subject to change without notice. Prices do not include applicable taxes. Sales tax applicable in N.Y. Canadian residents will be charged applicable taxes. Offer not valid in Quebec. This offer is limited to one order per household. All orders subject to credit approval. Credit or debit balances in a customer's account(s) may be offset by any other outstanding balance owed by or to the customer. Please allow 4 to 6 weeks for delivery. Offer available while quantities last.

Your Privacy—The Reader Service is committed to protecting your privacy. Our Privacy Policy is available online at www.ReaderService.com or upon request from the Reader Service.

We make a portion of our mailing list available to reputable third parties that offer products we believe may interest you. If you prefer that we not exchange your name with third parties, or if you wish to clarify or modify your communication preferences, please visit us at www.ReaderService.com/consumerchoice or write to us at Reader Service Preference Service, P.O. Box 9062, Buffalo, NY 14269. Include your complete name and address.

FAMOUS FAMILIES

YES! Please send me the *Famous Families* collection featuring the Fortunes, the Bravos, the McCabes and the Cavanaughs. This collection will begin with 3 FREE BOOKS and 2 FREE GIFTS in my very first shipment— and more valuable free gifts will follow! My books will arrive in 8 monthly shipments until I have the entire 51-book *Famous Families* collection. I will receive 2-3 free books in each shipment and I will pay just $4.49 U.S./$5.39 CDN for each of the other 4 books in each shipment, plus $2.99 for shipping and handling.* If I decide to keep the entire collection, I'll only have paid for 32 books because 19 books are free. I understand that accepting the 3 free books and gifts places me under no obligation to buy anything. I can always return a shipment and cancel at any time. My free books and gifts are mine to keep no matter what I decide.

268 HCN 9971   468 HCN 9971

Name _____ (PLEASE PRINT)

Address _____ Apt. # _____

City _____ State/Prov. _____ Zip/Postal Code _____

Signature (if under 18, a parent or guardian must sign)

Mail to the **Reader Service:**
IN U.S.A.: P.O. Box 1867, Buffalo, NY 14240-1867
IN CANADA: P.O. Box 609, Fort Erie, Ontario L2A 5X3

* Terms and prices subject to change without notice. Prices do not include applicable taxes. Sales tax applicable in N.Y. Canadian residents will be charged applicable taxes. This offer is limited to one order per household. All orders subject to approval. Credit or debit balances in a customer's account(s) may be offset by any other outstanding balance owed by or to the customer. Please allow 4 to 6 weeks for delivery. Offer available while quantities last. Offer not available to Quebec residents.

Your Privacy- The Reader Service is committed to protecting your privacy. Our Privacy Policy is available online at www.ReaderService.com or upon request from the Reader Service.
We make a portion of our mailing list available to reputable third parties that offer products we believe may interest you. If you prefer that we not exchange your name with third parties, or if you wish to clarify or modify your communication preferences, please visit us at www.ReaderService.com/consumerschoice or write to us at Reader Service Preference Service, P.O. Box 9062, Buffalo, NY 14269. Include your complete name and address.

FFBPA11

13.0